The Game

The Game

Izzy Abrahami

Tough Poets Press
Arlington, Massachusetts

ISBN 978-0-578-96431-7

This edition published with permission from
the Estate of Izzy Abrahami in 2021 by:

Tough Poets Press
Arlington, Massachusetts 02476
U.S.A.

www.toughpoets.com

For Rivka,
who game me lots of courage to leave
the Game.
And for Enid.

Contents

The Game

The Watching Couple

The balcony of the Balcony Man was the only escape from an unhappy marriage. He had always known that marriage was a voyage from which no traveler returned happy. But he was married! A point of no return.

That night, the TV set irritated him and his wife. The picture kept going on and off and black lines would cover the screen. And it happened especially during the most suspense-filled film of the week, a horror movie called *Light in the Darkness*. His wife became very angry when the picture went off for the tenth time. And she blamed him! Furious, he went to the balcony.

Standing there, watching the apartments opposite him, he discovered some things of interest. He saw thousands of windows in the many buildings, and in the windows lights were being switched on and off. The seventy-two ten-storey apartment buildings in the housing development were precisely alike, and from his balcony (his building was on a hill) he could see nearly all of them. The appearances and disappearances of the lights created a constant glittering. On and off, on and off. He wondered that he had not noticed the phenomenon before.

Suddenly he discovered that the patches of light and dark in the windows were creating patterns. Every minute the patterns changed as the people living behind the windows fulfilled their minute-to-minute needs.

He stood there, stunned, looking at the lights.

He started to play.

He told himself: if this window lights up while I am counting to ten, then I shall run away from home and from my wife. If not—that's that. If the light in that window goes out within a count of ten—my wife still loves me. If the light in another window goes on during a count of ten, I should get the hell out of here.

It seemed very childish at first, but after a while he found himself questioning about his past, present, and future, questioning about his friends, and relations, his work, his loves and hates. Once he even tried the theme of whether the girl he had loved at twenty-three still remembered him. The window did light up during his count of five (he had made the chances smaller by counting to five instead of ten), and it meant that she did remember him. He wondered what meeting her now would be like. He had loved her so much and so completely. Now he felt he still loved her. He would have given anything to meet her again.

He tried to lessen the chances even more. On a piece of paper he drew the blocks of flats opposite and made up some rules.

The first rule was that if during a count of fifty, the top corner right windows in at least seven blocks were lit, the answer to any question would be YES.

He went on to make ten elementary rules of play, bringing in different subjects, concerning the important phases of his life. It seemed that he was going to construct a new complete and unabridged version of His Life and Loves.

The future, according to the results, seemed quite interesting and promising. To the question of whether he would meet the girl he so dearly loved, the constellation of lights in the windows answered: YES WITH POSITIVE RESULTS.

In the next few days, the Balcony Man and his wife did not talk to each other. She went on watching and banging the television set. He was on the balcony by early evening, as soon as it started to get dark.

He made more rules.

A few times, he tried to get the answer: LOTS OF SEX AND LOVE OUTSIDE MARRIAGE IN THE COMING YEAR. But failed. Instead he got: BE PASSIVE. DON'T PUSH IT, IT WILL COME TO YOU.

He had constructed the game in such a way that during an evening he could get a story like this:

"She loves you. And how! Without reservations. You will meet her and positive results will emerge from this meeting. You will have lots of love and sex, but you must be active!"

But he was very puzzled when the story he actually got was both funny and absurd:

YOUR JOB WILL NOT IMPROVE. THE BOSS DOES NOT LIKE YOU. YOU WILL NOT CHANGE YOUR JOB. BUT YOU ARE GOING TO MAKE IT. THIS WILL LEAD TO LOVE AND SEX OUTSIDE MARRIAGE. YOU SHOULD BE ACTIVE. YOU WILL QUIT YOUR JOB AND MOVE TO A VILLA NEAR A RIVER.

How on earth could he not change his job and at the same time quit his job? How was he going to make it if his job is not going to improve? How absurd!

The next evening, three times in succession he got this: YOU WILL NOT LEAVE YOUR WIFE IN THE COMING FIVE YEARS. To his question whether he would do it at any other time the lights went mad and did not create any combination that fitted any of his rules. In other words, he would not. He felt lost. The only happy thing for him was that to his question whether he was lost or not the answer was, YOU ARE NOT!

At one time during the late evening he looked into his room where he saw his wife leaning over the television set, banging it madly, hopelessly trying to bring the absent picture back.

When The Game appeared to him it was already midnight. He felt like the captain of a lost ship discovering a bit of land. Feverishly, he began to draw a diagram of the buildings and windows he could see. He found a pair of dice, threw it, and placed two tokens on the diagram. Ten. Move ten windows! He landed on a lighted window—lose two points, go forward three windows. He threw the dice again. Nine. Move nine windows. He landed on a dark window—win three points, move back five windows. He threw the dice again. Two!

By five in the morning he had completed the construction of The Game and had made its rules.

Marriage was not a bad thing after all. At seven o'clock he told his wife that she should never watch television again, as it was more or less ruining their lives. Instead, he offered her a better form of amusement.

She flew into a temper, thinking he was trying to deprive her, apart from everything else, of the joy of the little square box, too.

"Never!" she shrieked.

"But I'm trying to show you a better pastime."

"I don't want to hear of it! You're cruel. Why did I ever meet you? You want to take from me my only pleasure!"

"But it's a game, like watching thousands of televisions."

"What do you mean thousands of televisions? You never had enough money to buy a color TV. You don't even care for your job . . ."

"I promise you thousands of televisions through which you can see real life . . ."

"How can you promise a thing like that?"

"If you'll listen I'll tell you."

"Listen to you? You've promised me so much and what do I have? Nothing, absolutely nothing. The neighbors have a thousand times more than we have."

"How do you know?"

"I imagine. I know."

"But why can't you see the life of all the neighbors and get it straight once and for all?"

"How on earth can I do that?"

"By the game."

"What game?"

Then he told her about The Game.

The Gentleman Who First Discovered the Watching Couple

The Gentleman Who First Discovered the Watching Couple fixed his eyes on the balcony opposite his own. Standing in the dark room, hidden behind the window curtain, in astonishment he followed the couple's every move. For two nights the Watching Couple had been sitting on their balcony, watching and pointing at the apartments opposite them, exchanging remarks and making notes.

The previous night they had pointed directly at his flat. Should he tell his wife, he wondered. She'd hit the roof.

Now the Watching Couple clearly were gazing and pointing at him! Point-blank. That frightened him beyond reason. Why were they doing it? He hadn't done anything wrong.

That evening he quarreled with his wife. Too preoccupied with the Watching Couple, he had refused to watch his favorite program, *Light in the Darkness*, on television. To his wife, nothing short of a holocaust could justify such a thing.

Almost mesmerized, he continued to peer at the Watching Couple. His sense of justice told him that watching the Watching Couple was no less of a moral offense than that of the Watching Couple watching him. But tearing himself from his post was more than he could do.

Even at his tiny office in the city, he could not escape the feeling that people from the neighboring office building were watching him. He did not see them watching, but how could he be sure that they were not watching him while he was not watching them? Consequently, he refused to take off his jacket and tie during work, which made some secretaries giggle.

At one point he found himself counting the windows he could see from his office. Three thousand, two hundred windows. From my apartment I can see much more, he thought, and cursed the architects of the housing development.

That evening he went to see his friend who worked at the post office of the housing development. The sitting room window in the apartment of the Gentleman from the Post did not face the balcony of the Watching Couple. But soon when using the toilet the Gentleman Who First Discovered the Watching Couple discovered that from its window one had almost a direct line to the balcony! Every now and then he excused himself, put on his jacket and tie, and went to the toilet to have a look at the couple watching the apartments opposite. At one point he thought he might even share with the Gentleman from the Post his discovery of the Watching Couple, but at once rejected the idea. The Watching Couple was his! It occurred to him that everyone should have his own Watching Couple.

The Gentleman from the Post had never seen anything like it. To dress up for the toilet! "Maybe it is the new in thing in the city," he thought.

But later, when the Gentleman Who First Discovered the Watching Couple returned from his sixth visit to the toilet, he broke down and told him the story of the Watching Couple.

"Put on your jacket," insisted the GD.

"I will not," said the GP.

"It's for your own good."

"I refuse."

"Do you refuse to come to the toilet?"

"I don't mind the toilet, but I refuse to dress up for it."

"But they are watching us!"

"Without jacket!"

They sneaked to the toilet, and looked through the window. The shocked GP rapidly brought a small pair of opera glasses and they took turns using it to watch the Watching Couple.

Nothing on the opposite balcony had changed. The Watching Couple were still pointing at certain apartments, writing things down and exchanging remarks. The GP almost blushed when they obviously gazed at his toilet window, pointed at him, and wrote him down.

They could not tear themselves away. The GP asked the GD to stay the night at his place. The GD refused. He could not leave his wife alone at such a horrifying time, but on the other hand thought that staying overnight in a bachelor's apartment, most probably in the toilet, might be interpreted wrongly. But he promised he would drop in in the morning. Something had to be done. That was sure. But they decided to wait a few days before deciding on their course of action.

Coming home the GD found his wife fast asleep. He lay on his bed, eyes open. What a strange world, he thought. A small square on the opposite side can change one's whole life.

The next morning the GD rushed to the apartment of the GP as promised. The door was unlocked and no one seemed to be around. He made for the toilet. On a makeshift chair the GP, his jacket on, was happily snoring. The GD could not resist the temptation and flushed the water. The GP jumped in panic. "It wasn't funny," he said after catching his breath.

"I didn't mean to frighten you."

"It's not joke-time," he declared energetically. "Hard times lie ahead. At exactly two o'clock the Watching Couple turned off their lights. Eventually they went to sleep. Or, what I am more inclined to believe, gave the impression of going to sleep."

"You slept here?"

"No, sir," said the GP. "I did not sleep. I would not think of deserting my post."

"I have to go to work," said the GD while making for the door.

For the first time in years the GD was late to his office. He could not work. The Watching Couple haunted him. The GD did not think he was panicky, but he certainly thought so of the GP, who in turn thought just the opposite. But whatever they thought of each other, they were bound together now by the Watching Couple.

After work the GD rushed to the apartment of the GP. At once they went to the toilet—and were stunned.

The Watching Couple now had two large pairs of binoculars. The men in the toilet cringed, sure of being spotted this time. Again, the couple were clearly watching, exchanging comments and writing them down.

How is it possible that the other people in the development haven't noticed them, the GD thought.

By now the GP was sitting on the floor out of sight of the Watching Couple. The GD felt an urge to go home. "I am going," he said, "but I'll be back."

Entering his flat the GD found it surprisingly dark. All of a sudden his wife, shaking all over, jumped onto him and dragged him to the floor. He knew at once she had noticed the Watching Couple.

There was a knock on the door. They decided in whispers not

to open it, but hearing the voice of their neighbor from downstairs, they did.

Within the hour all the neighbors from their entryway were assembled in their bathroom and kitchen, where the windows did not face the balcony of the Watching Couple. By then everybody had already seen the Watching Couple with their "huge" binoculars—watching and spying. The bathroom and the kitchen area were crammed full and noisy. No one knew exactly why they had come, who had invited them, or what was the purpose of the gathering. The GD's wife was coming back to life. Pushing her way through the guests, she greeted everybody and exchanged impressions of the Watching Couple. There had not been such a gathering in her house since the day of her marriage and the presence of so many people excited her. She went to the other room, changed, and reappeared.

Everybody was discussing the Watching Couple. People whose common past was no more than three hundred good-mornings down the elevator were now gladly talking to each other. Everybody had something to say about the situation.

"Why don't we call the police, and put an end to it?"

"Because they might be the police."

"Then they must be after something."

"The police are always after something."

"Now, let me ask you, if they're the police, what's all the fuss about?"

"Because, suppose they are not the police?"

"If they're not the police, there is reason to worry, but then we can't call them because they might be the police. Is that it?"

"Sure."

"And if they're the police, there's no reason to worry, and then there's no need to call them. Is that it?"

"So what the hell are they watching us for?"

"There're many other possibilities besides the police."

"They can be sex maniacs."

"I'm sure they are!"

"Isn't that terrible. What people can indulge in nowadays!"

"It might be more than that!"

"What do you mean?"

"They might be official income tax spies and at the same time assigned by the police to gather information."

"That leaves out sex, thank God."

"Not necessarily. An official can be a sex maniac as well as an official."

"Speaking about spies, why should the government want to spy on its own people?"

"They might be spies of another government."

"Can't be, they wouldn't do it as openly as that."

"Why not? That's the safest method for spying."

"They can be easily caught."

"They can always confess to being sex maniacs. It carries less penalty."

"What can they spy about here?"

"I'm getting the creeps."

"They want to give us the creeps."

"But what for? What for?"

"They like it."

"But why?"

"Power!"

"They might well be Israeli commandos."

"What!"

"Trying to trace a war criminal who just might be living in the housing development."

"No. No one here speaks with a foreign accent."

"But maybe the Watching Couple are foreigners."

"They must be foreigners. Only foreigners can do a thing like that."

"Please, please, we should keep to the facts. Didn't somebody say they were Israelis? So they must be foreigners. I haven't seen an Israeli who was not a foreigner."

"When you say Israeli, do you mean Jewish?"

"Please, do stop confusing the issue!"

"Isn't it frightening. We are all getting panicked."

"It means only one thing, that if they had good intentions we wouldn't be in a panic."

"Who told you they have any intentions at all?"

"Only a lunatic would do a thing like that with no intentions."

"This leaves the possibility that they are lunatics."

"Then we could call the police."

"I wouldn't advise it."

"Why not?"

"They might be the police!"

All of a sudden an old man who was standing in the middle of the bathtub started to shout:

"Who is the host here? Who is the host here?"

Some people pointed at the Gentleman Who First Discovered the Watching Couple who was making his way to the old man.

"Can I help you?"

"Who is the host here?"

"I am the host."

"Then you must know what's going on here."

"Don't you know what's going on?"

"How should I know? I am not the host. Who is the host?"

"I am the host."

"Then for the love of Christ, can you tell me what's going on here?" said the old man.

The Gentleman Who First Discovered the Watching Couple became suspicious. He sensed that the Watching Couple was somehow dictating the events in the flats opposite to them and thought that this man might be a part of an unknown plot.

"You don't live on our block, do you?"

"No. Building thirty-seven, entrance I, apartment ninety-one. Three blocks away."

"Then how did you know about it?"

"About what?"

"What was going on here."

"That's it. What's going on here?"

The Gentleman Who First Discovered the Watching Couple felt that he was caught in a madman's illogical labyrinth. His sense of responsibility toward his wife and his neighbors made him lead the old man to the other room. "Take care not to be spotted," he said, pointing at the Watching Couple. "That's what's going on in here."

The old man was making for the balcony. The GD thought that if anyone dared to walk openly to the balcony he must have gone crazy. The old man was standing in the middle of the balcony almost in tears. "I can still make it. By God, I can still make it," he whispered. He entered the room. "Excuse me, I must go," he said and left swiftly. Reaching his apartment he went at once to his desk and started composing letters which were to be delivered to all the inhabitants of the housing development. It seems that the binoculars sale scheme had occurred to him. The GD could not have known about it. Nor could he have known the identity of the Lonely Gentleman.

The seventy-three people in the bathroom and the kitchen had already decided to go to the Gentleman from the Bar, as he would probably know the Watching Couple and could guess their reason for doing whatever they were doing. Leaving the flat in small groups not to attract attention, they saw some other people heading toward the bar.

The Gentleman from the Bar had already closed his doors,

and they had to identify themselves before he would let them in. They had to tell him, through the keyhole, their names, the numbers of their buildings, the letters of their entrances, and the numbers of their apartments. Everyone seemed to accept this strange practice in entering a bar as natural to the circumstances. The bar was packed. A hastily sketched diagram of the housing development was hanging on the wall.

After the disorder caused by their arrival and by the arrival of some other neighbors, the Gentleman from the Bar asked each one of them to speak up and tell of his experience concerning the Balcony Crisis.

Before speaking up, each one pointed at the diagram of the housing development and showed where his flat was situated, in order to trace the exact relation between his flat and the balcony of the Watching Couple.

It was apparent by now that the people gathered there were beginning to fly on the wings of their suddenly awakened imagination. Everything began to soar out of proportion and out of logic. The people happily dramatized and melodramatized.

Everyone told more or less the same story: the Watching Couple, the things they wrote down, the binoculars. To the question, what was the reason for the Watching Couple's tracking them down, people had very strange answers indeed. Russian spies, Chinese spies, someone even thought that they had to be Israeli commandos. Other suggestions were—sex maniacs, government spies, lunatics, tax spies, spies for an insurance company, to mention only a few.

Before he rose to speak, the Gentleman Who First Discovered the Watching Couple noticed that the Gentleman from the Post was sitting in a corner, pale and frightened, drinking a glass of beer. A woman had fainted but was revived at once with cold water.

The Gentleman Who First Discovered the Watching Couple

began his speech with: "As you all probably know I am the Gentleman Who First Discovered the Watching Couple . . ."

It worked. From that moment on everybody knew that he was the Gentleman Who First Discovered the Watching Couple.

His wife told him he had done well.

In an hour, the gathering which had started as an emergency meeting became spontaneously a happy party. People who were strangers before hugged each other, clinked glasses, sang "Victoria," "John Brown's Body" and the national anthem. A young actor recited Whitman's "I Hear America Singing" and a retired politician quoted the Thirteenth Amendment to the Constitution. "We Shall Overcome" and "Jesus Christ Superstar" followed.

In the end they decided to wait a few days to see if things would work themselves out. They were asked to leave the bar one by one. Some people approached the GD and his wife, and asked permission to watch the Watching Couple from their apartment, as they could not watch them from their own. They had only heard about them and had never actually seen them in action. The GD agreed.

Two women went to his apartment to watch the Watching Couple. They were scared stiff at seeing the real thing. The GD had to call the doctor from entrance A to give them some tranquilizers.

Through the small kitchen window he could see the other side of the housing development and the many people who were sneaking to their windows in the dark to watch the Watching Couple. One thing constantly troubled him. The Watching Couple weren't even trying to hide what they were doing!

The Game

When the Balcony Man told his wife about The Game she was excited.

They spent the whole of that day discussing The Game. They talked for hours, exchanging views on different aspects until they agreed on its basic principles and made the final rules.

For a few nights they played The Game according to the rules they had created. As his wife expressed herself, "We have tested The Game and its rules." They had indeed. It was heaven. No quarrels, no fights, just happiness and play. His wife was totally in love with the game.

Coming home from work the Balcony Man was given a warm welcome from his wife, a thing unusual in their marriage till then. She wasted no time in announcing triumphantly that the rules of the game as they had constructed them were "too simple and were making the game boring." That was the last thing the Balcony Man was expecting and he became terrified of what might become of their marriage, should the game be spoiled or stopped.

She handed him a piece of paper on which new rules were

written.

He was angry. He had hurried home to play the game, and now all of a sudden, new rules, new discussions, new quarrels.

But reading further he grew more interested. The additions basically supplemented the original rules. The idea was that the game should be played not only with the light and dark windows but also with the interiors of the apartments. It said that when a player "landed" on a lighted window, he was to look inside it, preferably with binoculars, as one could see more details that way. This would open up new possibilities in the game.

For whatever one saw inside the various apartments one gained or lost points. His wife had arranged it in such a way that the unusual won and the usual lost.

He read:

WHAT A PLAYER SHOULD SEE INSIDE THE VARIOUS APARTMENTS IN ORDER TO WIN OR LOSE POINTS:

To Win:

A man, woman, or child	1 point each
A Negro	15 points
Kissing couple	7 points
Television off	12 points
Animals other than cats, dogs, or cage-birds	13 points
Birthday party (over and above one point for each person present)	5 points
Sexual intercourse (between people)	32 points
An adult reading a book	3 points
If the title of the book is visible:	
Fiction	6 points
Non-fiction	4 points
Poetry	63 points

Drama	109 points
James Joyce . . . . . . A Joker	Wins the game!
Naked Man	6 points
Half-naked man (no matter which half)	4 points

To Lose:

Television on	19 points
Couple fighting	9 points
Cats or dogs	5 points each
People playing cards	7 points
Apartment being cleaned	7 points
Windows being cleaned	6 points
An adult reading a newspaper	96 points
If the newspaper is recognizable:	
Daily News	23 points
Time Magazine	19 points
Playboy	7 points
National Geographic	10 points
Screw Magazine	56 points
Good Housekeeping	55 points
Wall Street Journal	3 points
Christian Science Monitor	54 points
Half-naked woman (upper half)	73 points
Half-naked woman (lower half)	6 points

The next day was a day to remember for the Balcony Man. In the morning his wife brought him coffee in bed and sat down beside him. Opening his eyes he could hardly believe it. But it was not a dream. She said she was happy! That was something he had not heard for a long time. She said it was a beautiful morning, which rang in his ears as if it were a brilliant piece of poetry. She said she would like to meet him in the city after work so they could go together and choose binoculars for their game with its new rules.

To his objection that they simply could not afford to buy such things, she produced a thick wad of money which, she explained apologetically, she had been keeping for a rainy day.

It was a crazy afternoon.

They went to many shops in town to make inquiries and get advice on the kind of binoculars they should buy. The first thing each clerk wanted to know was the purpose for which they needed the binoculars. At first they told about the game, but somehow no one took it as a game. The next store they entered, the clerk was very puzzled.

"Do you mean watching other people's apartments?"

"Right."

"Seriously?"

"No. We told you it was a game."

"Watching other people's interiors?"

"It can be very funny."

"I'll have to have a word with the manager."

The manager appeared. "I'm awfully sorry but I can't sell binoculars to be used for voyeuristic purposes. It's against the law."

The Watching Couple started to giggle.

"Well," the manager added, "I don't blame you. After all we're all human, aren't we?" He winked at the Balcony Man and disappeared.

After a few more such misunderstandings they stopped that practice. Finally, at another store, the Balcony Man said that they were going to hunt lions in Africa and needed two pairs of the best and clearest binoculars, with the most powerful lenses available. They got them. And they paid a fortune. The clerk's only comment was, "Lions? Isn't it better to sit at home and watch your neighbors?"

Come evening, the Watching Couple were already sitting on their balcony with the new set of rules and new binoculars, playing the game.

It is hardly possible to describe the pleasure they had that evening. For the first time since their wedding they felt intimate and happy. They laughed at the small incidents they saw in the various flats, they were astonished and thrilled by others, they often grew curious and tried to guess the outcome of quarrels between young couples. They felt pathetically romantic seeing an old couple embracing and kissing.

They ran their binoculars from one apartment to another not to miss a single experience. Through the glasses the other side seemed like an enormous theater where nine thousand and one hundred dramas, comedies, tragedies, melodramas, and plays of the absurd were silently being played on nine thousand and one hundred different stages. The Balcony Man and his wife had the feeling that they were in it, actually present and participating in the life experiences of others, and at the same time outside it. It added another romantic dimension to their excitement.

"Oh, look. Look over there!" cried the Balcony Man's wife. "They're undressing, can you see?"

"She's beautiful."

"Do you think they're married?"

"Why not?"

"Should we go on watching them? They'll be naked in a minute."

"I'll be damned! They're in two different neighboring apartments."

"That's right! They're so near each other."

"They can't be more than three feet apart."

"They make nearly the same movements undressing. It's almost like a dance."

"Imagine that the wall suddenly collapsed."

"They couldn't wish for a better introduction."

"It looks so funny. Especially when they face each other."

"There, see? Seven windows to the right, two rows down!"

"Praying before dinner, aren't they?"
"Is the man with the beard a rabbi?"
"He might be."
"I've never seen a rabbi before."
"Two to the left they are praying too."
"We've never prayed before dinner."
"Hey, come back one window. See between the two windows of the praying families?"
"What's that?"
"Projecting blue movies on the wall! Can't you see?"
"Isn't it pathetic?"

Through their binoculars the Watching Couple could see now the three apartments at once. The naked bodies on the wall performing almost all possible ways of sexual intercourse were sandwiched between the two God-fearing families.

"See that toilet window there?"
"Oh God. What would two men want to do in a toilet?"
"A gay party."
"Oh, is it?"
"Look, they have some sort of binoculars too."
"That doesn't fit a gay party, does it?"
"You never know."
"It's a kind of opera glasses."
"Do you think they might be playing our game?"
"Can't be. They wouldn't know the rules."
"Maybe they have a different set of rules."
"Hey, move eleven to the left, three down."
"I can't make it out, what is he doing?"
"He's either rehearsing a speech or he's an actor."
"I think he is an actor. He's standing on a chair."
"In his underpants?"
"In his apartment, why not?"
"Now look carefully. It's hilarious, see the next apartment to

the left?"

"Three old couples watching television. Nothing exciting."

"Try to ignore the TV set, doesn't it look as if the old couples were his audience?"

"Unbelievable!"

"Nothing ever happens in there."

"Where?"

"Eighteen to the right, two up."

"Still talking."

"They must be quite young."

"His new date, maybe."

"What are they talking so much about?"

"Analyzing? Trying to find themselves?"

From the Watching Couple's point of view it seemed ridiculous. The beautiful young couple on the opposite side were talking for hours as if they did not know that eighteen windows to the right a man was beating his wife, twenty-eight and twenty-nine windows further a man and a woman were undressing to go to bed and not together, five rows down a woman was breast-feeding her newly born baby, the actor or the executive was making his speech in his underpants to an imaginary audience, and nineteen windows to the right a very old woman was lying in bed motionless and unattended. The young beautiful couple went on talking while thirty-seven windows to the left and five rows down an old couple was embracing and kissing in their kitchen.

The Balcony Man wondered what would happen if by some miracles all the walls of the houses collapsed, and the people could see this wide-angle panoramic view.

It dawned upon him that he and his wife were only a small detail of that huge kinetic canvas spread out before them. Confronted with all the stages and phases of life being acted out in the flats opposite, he felt how absurd it was not to be in love all the time, not to be happy all the time. How meaningless their fights over money and television had been. Time was running on, very fast, running with the lights from window to window.

All of a sudden his binoculars froze on a window. A young girl was sitting on the floor, apparently listening to a record. Didn't he know her? She looked much the same as his memory of his girl from his past. Past? He was to meet her. Wasn't he? That was what the windows had indicated a few nights before. He hadn't seen her for three years. Was she still alone? Three years ago she was. When he came she was not. When he left she was again.

He could not take his eyes from her. It was not she, but she was his memory of her.

Looking at her, he felt he had made a mess of it all. Suddenly he realized that he had never done what he wanted to do, that he had never rested when he had wanted to rest, and had never run when he had wanted to run. Now he felt he wanted to live many lives in one, make lifelong mistakes and never regret them, and always come back when he wanted to. Instead he had married a wife at twenty-five and gotten a steady job, had never made big mistakes but always regretted it, had never wanted to stay where he had been staying but always came back.

The girl on the opposite side was now changing a record. Her whole body was in full view.

The Balcony Man was in love.

He looked at his wife. She was watching the apartments with her binoculars as if turning every block inside out. Was she feeling the same? She was relaxed and her face was tender and soft. He had never seen her like this. All her hardness and stiffness had disappeared.

He sensed that this huge, blocklike, four-dimensional manifestation of life was working on them both. What was the importance of working, toiling, quarreling, fighting, winning or being beaten, accumulating or losing money, when one was subjected to a certain order which it was not in one's power to change?

Work was no fun for the Balcony Man during the next day. He waited for the evening to come as he had never done before, not even in the early days of his marriage. All his thoughts during the day were directed toward the game and what he had experienced the night before. He would have loved to see the people he worked with through his binoculars when they were alone or with their families.

The Watching Couple were already on the balcony by early evening, playing the game. Looking at the opposite side he saw her. She was there too. The girl of yesterday. Alone.

Later in the evening, his wife noticed several binoculared men on the opposite side. She explained enthusiastically that they were going to add another rule to the game.

The new rule was that if a player landed on a lighted window where he saw a person with binoculars he was to get twelve points. Each man with binoculars in a dark window—three points.

The Balcony Man agreed. It made the game even better.

Indeed, while playing the game, the Balcony Man and his wife saw, in other windows, people with binoculars watching. In a while there was quite a lot of people with binoculars. The Balcony Man was beginning to wonder if all of them were playing the game, though with a different set of rules from his. He told his wife about this with some uneasiness. She dismissed it completely.

The Balcony Man accepted the new scene as part of the game, and as a fact which, according to the new rule his wife had created, was a winner. Toward the end of the evening, the new rule began working in his favor. At one point he decided to go back and landed on a lighted window where a man with binoculars was watching. He got twelve points. His wife was not very pleased. The new rule she herself had so enthusiastically introduced was now turning cruelly against her.

He decided not to let new rules into the game so easily. In the hope that his wife would win the game in the following evenings he went to bed.

The Big Rush

The day after the meeting in the bar, when the Gentleman Who First Discovered the Watching Couple came back from work, many people in the housing development greeted him warmly, most unusual practice in the area. He could sense a kind of unity among the people. Everybody seemed to know him. Only the day before he had been completely unknown.

When finally he got home, his wife, in an alarming state of terror, handed him an envelope still unopened. On it, in big black letters, was written: "For the Head of the Family Only. Top secret." And in smaller letters: "Strict orders! Not to be opened by anyone else but the head of the family."

His wife clung to him. He drew her firmly to him, and felt her heart beating.

The letter, handwritten, said:

Dear Flat Dweller,

Owing to the grave situation and the alarming state of affairs which we face today in our housing development, created by the Watching Couple, we have secretly elected a select committee from among our Estate Troopers, to meet the great need of the hour. They are authorized to issue orders, to mobilize reserves at short notice, to decide on the nationalization of property. Their first task has been to declare a state of emergency. A state of mobilization will follow.

At the moment they are planning a curfew, which will shortly be imposed on our citizens and their families.

The names of the select committee must remain secret. Nevertheless, they have issued the following declaration:

We are no longer prepared to tolerate the reign of terror imposed on us, and we call upon our standard-bearers to prepare themselves for our long struggle!

We will fight on the balconies, we will fight at the windows, we will fight on the roofs. We will launch a full-scale attack with high militant spirit and under martial law. Strict discipline is a must.

Let us have no deserters in this great hour!

Everyone is a volunteer and together we are a unity which cannot be defeated!

Have trust in us!

The GD was trembling by the time he had finished reading the letter. He had a feeling somebody was playing a dirty trick on him. He recognized in the letter broken quotations from Churchill and amateurish war phrases which sounded as if they had been taken from a second-rate dictionary. But was he frightened! And he knew there were good reasons for his fear. Glancing over the letter again he found a P.S.:

Top secret!
Observe and be on guard! Report EVERYTHING suspicious!
Sacrifices will have to be made! Be ready!
Make your decision NOW!

Binoculars leave nothing to the imagination!

Between the many cares and worries of that moment, he caught a glimpse of the Watching Couple watching and talking to each other very enthusiastically, and alas, pointing at him.

War was openly declared! Some of his neighbors started knocking on his door.

Everything seemed to go out of hand. But not altogether.

What seemed to have happened was that the manager of one of the big supermarkets in the housing development, after having received the emergency letter, called his boss in the city and explained to him what was going on in the area. He suggested that they open the supermarket even though it was late at night. He was convinced, he said, "that people in these circumstances are prepared to buy everything. This," he said, was his "unique opportunity to bring to the open his potential insight into the psychology of shoppers." The boss agreed. The moment the manager followed his "insight" and opened the supermarket and put on full lights, other stores, getting the message, followed suit. The opportunity to sell was at hand.

A red-eyed woman rushed into the apartment of the Gentleman Who First Discovered the Watching Couple and declared that the food stores of the housing development were opening. This would not have been so strange had it not been nine o'clock at night. There were two huge supermarkets in the area and about seven small food stores.

In a few minutes, hundreds, if not thousands, were already rushing toward the food stores, the gas stations, the banks, and the cigarette shops, all of which were now open. People were running along with bags to fill up with goods while they were still available.

The GD's wife completely recovered from her shock and, forgetting the letter altogether, asked her husband to take a jerrycan and buy five gallons of gasoline. As they did not have a car it seemed a little strange to buy gas. But that, his wife explained, was a very naïve assumption; money can always lose its value but gasoline can always be exchanged for food.

At the start of the Big Rush people tried to avoid being in the view of the Watching Couple who were doing nothing but binoculing them all around.

But in a short while no one cared whether they were spotted as long as they could stock up for the dark days fast approaching.

There were shoals of people streaming to and fro, many already lining up for the third or tenth time to get more of everything. Although all the houses in the area had central heating, people panicked and ran toward two recently arrived trucks carrying coal, and in a couple of minutes everything in them had been bought, including, alas, some personal belongings of the drivers. Coal trucks kept arriving all through the night.

As he was standing in the long line for sugar, the spirit of the people seemed for a moment to hover in front of the GD, and set his emotions awhirl.

All night thousands of people, like ants, were preparing themselves for what appeared to be a dark and cold winter. Many were carrying cartloads of goods and others were dragging sacks full of food, coal, and clothes. At one point the GD saw the Gentleman from the Post slowly wandering about among thousands of moving bodies. His face was almost expressionless. As the GP passed along the line the GD touched him gently. He shuddered and stopped. The GD invited him to join him in the line although it was contrary to the ethics of the housing development. The GP shivered, refused the offer, and pointed toward the balcony of the couple. The GD could hardly believe his eyes. Only now did he realize that no one of the thousands of excited people cared about the couple or what they did! Events were taking their own special course. How else could he explain the fact that the balcony was empty!

The balcony was really and truly empty. The GP leaned toward the GD and whispered, "The police. I called the police! Now they are there! Inside. I'm sorry! I had to. The letter I got. I went out of my mind. You will explain. I haven't slept. You tell them, will you? I called them! They came. You can explain . . ." And with a deep sigh he wandered off.

At that moment three policemen walked out of the Watching Couple's block and headed toward their car. They did not seem to notice what was going on around them, and the people seemed to ignore their presence. The GD remained in line without having any notion what to do. He only thought it was a good thing that the free world had been notified.

The Free World Had Been Notified

From the Police Day-by-day Report:

Received a telephone call concerning a certain disorder in the area. The complaint: "A couple with binoculars are watching the flats opposite them."

Patrolman No. 7111 was sent to investigate the complaint.

Patrolman No. 7111 reports: "I found the person who had complained about the so-called 'Watching Couple' in a state of melancholy and fright. From his inconsistent statements I gathered that he was afraid of a couple who sat every evening on their balcony watching everybody, including himself, with 'huge binoculars.' They also wrote things down. He also said that many people had noticed it already, and that it was creating a great disturbance in the area.

"He confessed that he was not the one who first discovered the 'Watching Couple.' That, he said, was another man who lived only a few blocks away from him. They had both been keeping an eye on them for sometime. This was before the 'Watching Couple' were noticed by the public at large. He himself had been afraid to inform the police of the incident. He could not make the reason for this clear. He stated that the whole area was panic-stricken, as no one knew what was behind 'The Watching Affair.' He works in the post office and is known in the area as 'The Gentleman from the Post.'

"Although I think he is in constant fear and seems to be afraid of practically everything, and his words cannot be taken at face value, I recommend sending somebody to check on the so-called 'Watching Couple.'"

How Many Points for a Cop?

Alas! Just as the Balcony Man arrived home from work, he had the shock of his life. There was a knock on the door and a second later the police were there!

Three policemen with guns all but forced their way in. They wanted to know whether the couple had any binoculars. What a funny question! Of course they did.

And then, for two long hours the policemen tried to get out of him, and later, out of his wife, what they called "the truth." At first they seemed not to believe a word of what he told them about the game and how it all began. After some hours and after examining all the diagrams and drawings of the game, and after thoroughly searching the flat, they started to compare the things his wife had said with his story.

"You said you saw a man and a woman undressing. Is that correct?"

"Yes."

"Your wife said 'we have never seen anybody naked or even half naked.' How'd you explain that?"

The Balcony Man's wife said hurriedly, "When we saw them

starting to undress I told my husband to shut his eyes. I did, too."

"Did your husband shut his eyes?"

"Of course he did!"

"In your testimony, speaking of your marriage, you said: 'He had never done anything I wanted him to do.' How come all of a sudden he shut his eyes because you told him to do so?"

"Because he's better now."

"Did you shut your eyes when your wife told you to shut them?"

"No."

"So you saw them naked?"

"No, I had . . . already landed on another window and was going on with the game. So I didn't see anything."

Patrolman 7111 was annoyed. He did not know what to do. He could not lawfully arrest the Watching Couple, as watching from one's own apartment, even with binoculars, was not a violation of the law. He was convinced that no physical harm was intended and he could not find any indication of a moral offense. He was at a loss.

"You are under arrest," he said.

"What the hell," said the second patrolman, who had been patrolling the balcony during the questioning.

"What's wrong?" asked patrolman 7111.

"I see other guys are out with binoculars, too."

Patrolman 7111 stepped onto the balcony. He could clearly see that from some apartments on the opposite side a few people were watching with binoculars.

"What the hell," said patrolman 7111, "I can't arrest the whole damn population, can I? O.K. No charges, we're off."

He took the other patrolman aside and whispered, "I want this goddamn game thoroughly investigated."

"How?"

"By playing it."

"It'll be a pleasure," said the patrolman.

By then the Balcony Man was so exhausted that he felt only half conscious.

Later his wife told him that he had kept on repeating, "Please, don't stop our game. Please, don't stop our game."

His wife proved tougher than he. She had even enjoyed the whole affair, she said later.

Before they left, one of the patrolman told her confidentially that they could not find a law against citizens innocently using binoculars on their own balconies. There were many people in town watching birds from their balconies with binoculars, they said.

That same patrolman surprisingly asked the Balcony Man's wife if he could come with his wife sometime and play the game with them. He had two pairs of large binoculars and he had never had the opportunity to use them. She was so surprised and embarrassed that she invited them around the following evening.

The Balcony Man only hoped this was no trick. They would have to wait and see.

"Tell me," the patrolman asked the Balcony Man, "how many points you get for spotting a cop?"

Bewildered by the sudden change, the Balcony Man could hardly think of an answer. He had never seen a cop in any of the apartments and there was no mention of a cop in the present set of rules.

"You win twenty points," he murmured.

"I'm glad," said the patrolman. "It's five points more than a Negro."

The next day the Balcony Man did not go to work, being so tired and still disturbed by what he had experienced the night before. Most of the day he stayed in bed and his wife took care of him in the most touching way.

As the evening was approaching his wife could not remember what time the patrolman and his wife were due to come, and neither of them could remember whether they were coming for dinner. The Watching Couple had to prepare dinner in order to avoid embarrassment. They were just finishing the preparations when the Balcony Man saw an envelope slipping beneath the door. He thought it was a late delivery.

The stenciled letter read:

> Dear flat dweller!
>
> We are all aware of the unusual activities and of the aggressive violation of human rights by the opposite side of our housing estate with respect to our side. We therefore warn every one of our men to be ready for the call at very short notice.
> We have carefully been following your noble activities during the last few days, especially your tireless and continuous observation of the other side.
> Get a service cap with a hatband.
> We believe in our troops!
> BE SOBER. ACCEPT THE CONSEQUENCES.
> Binoculars leave nothing to the imagination!

Remembering that the patrolman and his wife were to come to play the game, and also probably to have their dinner, the Balcony Man nearly panicked. His wife did not care much as long as they could go on playing the game.

They decided not to tell the Police Couple anything about the strange letter, which his wife called a hoax. For a moment the Balcony Man thought it was the police who were distributing these letters in order to test their innocence, but thinking further, he could find no real foundation for this assumption. Yet he did not rule it out entirely. Everything was possible.

Binoculars Leave Nothing to the Imagination

The Gentleman Who First Discovered the Watching Couple had thought the night before that events had reached their peak—never had he known such terror. But having gone through another day and another night he realized he had been wrong. The worst was still to come.

In the early evening, while his wife was still putting away the emergency supplies they had acquired the night before and he was watching the balcony of the Watching Couple anticipating their appearance, it happened.

He saw one of the patrolmen whom he recognized from the previous night, fully uniformed and accompanied by a woman—another official?—walking toward the entrance of the Watching Couple's block. This did not escape the notice of several others on his side. The next thing, he saw the patrolman and the woman sitting on the balcony together with the Watching Couple.

All of a sudden, all four of them produced large binoculars and with what seemed to be a mocking gesture started to watch their opposite side.

In a flash, the GD's entire side was galvanized into action. Tension mounted. It was already dark. The whole thing was beginning again, but this time with doubled force and doubled intensity. Everything seemed to be moving at such a speed that the GD did not even have time to consider his next step. He heard his wife scream. She was screaming at the sight of an envelope slipping, as if of its own accord, beneath the door. Opening the door carefully proved to the GD beyond doubt that the letter had indeed glided in by itself. Tearing open the envelope he found in it a short note which read:

> Fellow Citizen,
>
> As you have already seen, the authorities have joined the foe against us. This is it!
> War is declared!
> Woe to the eyes which see this!

While the GD and his wife were still wondering what it all meant, another note slipped beneath the door. This time he was faster and he just managed to catch a glimpse of the back of a man running down the stairs. His wife was growing more hysterical with each development. The new note read:

> Citizens,
>
> In our desperate situation we have contacted the below-listed stations, which will be ready within minutes to receive you. You are requested to contact them immediately in the following order:
> The control station.
> The depot.

The collecting station.
The frontier post.
The induction station.
The quarantine station.
The dressing station.
The outstation.
The repeater station.
The casualty clearing-house.
The subscriber station.
The sub-station.
The junction station.
The upstation.
Woe to the house whose eyes are open to the dark!
Remember, binoculars leave nothing to the imagination.

His wife and he sat down just inside the door to try to catch this energetic man of letters, if only to ask him how one would be expected to contact various stations, without even having the slightest idea of where these stations were. Now the GD knew that saboteurs and provocateurs were at work in an already critical situation.

The GD and his wife switched off all the lights and sat in the dark.

They could faintly hear screams from other flats. A light tap on the door was sufficient to make them jump. He flung the door open. There stood the Gentleman from the Post, his head bent, his arms limp. He said not a word. The GD's wife screamed, but the GP did not even react. They led him in. He sat down murmuring: "Thank you, thank you," and then cried out as if it was his last word: "Water." When they brought him his glass of water he would not drink it.

"That's it. I was expecting it," said the wife of the GD. "You didn't understand a word of what he said, did you?"

"For Christ sake, he said only one word: 'Water.'"

"And what does 'water' mean?"

"H_2O," said the GD.

"You are crazy," said his wife. "Water supplies will soon run out. That's what he meant!"

They could not confirm it, as the GP was already fast asleep.

Returning to the door the GD realized that he had missed his man of letters again. No one was outside. This note said:

> Citizen, remember,
>
> No common man that is not of the seed of our side should draw near!
> You have not followed the instructions of our last communication.
> Contact building 37, entrance I, apartment 91—tonight!

The GD no longer cared who was and who was not of the seed of his side or who in the name of God was sending all these notes. He was tired and envied the Gentleman from the Post snoring gently in his sleep.

For the first time in days he felt more at ease. Not that the situation had changed, but he was so tired that he could not stand it any longer. He went to the balcony to get some fresh air. On the opposite balcony the patrolman, the woman, and the young Watching Couple were still watching his side with their binoculars. Looking at the flats on his own side he suddenly noticed that some of the people were out on their balconies—watching the Watching Couple—with binoculars. It was so surprising that it hardly registered. But looking closely he noticed that the number of people was considerable. He only hoped his wife would not come, but, as he found out later, she was fast asleep.

He slipped out quietly and went toward building 37, entrance I. He had never before knocked at anybody's door as late as that.

But having no choice, he did it with determination. And courage.

Recognizing the man who opened the door cautiously, he was stunned. That was he! The Lonely Gentleman who had stood in the middle of the bathtub in his apartment. The same old man who had dared to go openly to the balcony facing the Watching Couple.

The Lonely Gentleman let him in and led him to his balcony. Picking up his binoculars the Lonely Gentleman continued to watch the Watching Couple in silence, ignoring his guest completely. The tension was so great that the GD needed the rest room urgently. It was very reassuring to know how to find it wherever one was, and one was sure to know, as all the apartments in the housing development were identical.

Coming back to the balcony with renewed confidence, and intrigued by the binoculars and their target, he asked the Lonely Gentleman to lend them to him for a moment in order to binocule the Watching Couple and their police guests.

Putting his binoculars down, the Lonely Gentleman gave him a pitiful look.

"You're a stranger, aren't you?"

"No. Not at all."

"Aren't you a foreigner?"

"No, why?"

"There's no such a verb in the English language like to binocule."

"I see."

"You could buy a pair if you wanted to."

"Do you sell them?"

"I certainly do."

"I'd like to have a pair."

"There's only one left. The last and the best. They leave nothing to the imagination."

The GD was bewildered. He knew this saying too well. Was he the man who was writing all these letters?

The Lonely Gentleman came back with the binoculars and handed them to him. He took them and patted them. They were huge and shining, and they cost a fortune. Only now did he realize that he could not escape any longer the present demands of the society he lived in. And he knew that the most urgent one was a pair of binoculars.

Showing him out, the Lonely Gentleman told him how to use the binoculars in the most effective way. Finally he expressed regret that he was one of the last nine people to buy the indispensable piece of equipment. Among the nine, he said, were six foreigners, one man in the hospital, another in a mental home, and he was the last. Pushing him out gently, he whispered, "I have to watch strangers, you know."

"I know," murmured the GD. "But all these letters, did you write all these letters?"

"Sure I did."

"But what for? What for?"

"Advertising."

"Advertising? Advertising what?"

"Binoculars," said the Lonely Gentleman and closed the door.

Never before had the GD been allowed to look into the lives of other people, to see into their kitchens, their sitting rooms—he even saw their bedrooms—to study their way of decorating their rooms, their style of living. He could see, in some of the apartments, pictures hanging on the walls, so good were his binoculars. He tried to guess whether they were originals or reproductions, as he regarded himself slightly informed on art. He saw their libraries, their television sets, their furniture. He could even pigeonhole the people living there and divide them into social groups. It was amazing.

All of a sudden he noticed that from other flats on their side many people were popping their heads out of their windows and running about as if in panic. Looking at his own side, which by now was fully equipped with everyone out on their balconies, with their shining binoculars, he could see why the other side was so panic-stricken. One by one their windows darkened. In a short while all their side was in darkness.

The Watch In

A knock on the door made the Balcony Man's heart beat faster. Joyfully, his wife went to open the door. The policeman and his wife came in. They had already dined but they would not mind joining for a small second dinner—during which the Balcony Man's wife explained to them the rules of the game. She had prepared two diagrams for their use. The policeman's wife thought that the game was too complicated, but the Watching Couple assured her that it only seemed so and that in playing it one discovered how simple it really was. They went to the balcony to start playing the game.

All of a sudden the Balcony Man noticed many people from the opposite side popping their heads out of their windows or appearing on their balconies, watching his own side with huge binoculars. It was obvious that they were not watching anything or anybody else but his balcony. He started to sweat. He looked at his wife. She looked back and smiled as if nothing were happening. He discovered that the patrolman and his wife thought that the people with the binoculars on the opposite side were also playing the game. They did not see anything unusual in it.

The new rule the Balcony Man's wife made up concerning people with binoculars only helped the Police Couple to regard what was happening opposite as part of the game.

They heard shouts and cries, mainly female, from the opposite side. On the spur of the moment, the Balcony Man's wife suggested some new rules for the game. It was to give points for the noises they could hear. That, she said, would make the game more interesting and definitely more musical. The patrolman regarded the shouts as normal night noises in an area where thousands of people were living. He was on his way to winning the game, and with a broad smile approved of the new rules. But the Balcony Man was so much against them that his wife agreed to postpone the change.

Going to the toilet, the Balcony Man found under the front door an envelope on which was written: "URGENT." Inside was a short note which read: "BLACKOUT! STAND BY!"

Coming back to the balcony he found the Police Couple and his wife going on with the game quite happily, not noticing a thing.

He looked at his own side. It was in total darkness. Not one window out of the thousands was lighted. Not knowing what he should do, he murmured that it might be better to play the game in the dark. "We could see the inside of the opposite flats much better," he grimly explained. His suggestion met with approval and he turned the lights off.

As he sensed that many strange events might follow, he wanted to get rid of his guests as soon as possible, and playing the game absent-mindedly he tried to find a reason to throw his guests out. His wife was not bothered by the total darkness on her side. She had not even noticed it.

All of a sudden the Balcony Man heard a slight knock on the door, which he tried to ignore. But the patrolman said there was a knock on the door.

Oh boy! The Balcony Man went trembling to the door. Opening it he found a short message:

> SALE! BINOCULARS FOR SALE. OPEN NOW. COME. DO NOT PUT IT OFF UNTIL TOMORROW. EXCLUSIVE BARGAINS. NUMEROUS MODELS AND MAKES.
>
> Building 37, entrance I, apartment 91. Ring once. Don't knock!
> Business as usual.
> Each family, or at least two of its members, should be within half an hour on their balconies with—BINOCULARS.
> The size of the binoculars has not been decided upon but they must be big enough not to leave anything to the imagination.
> Let them grope in the dark!
> And what I say unto you I say unto all: WATCH!
> He that is not with us is against us!
> Remember!
> Many that are first shall be last; and the last shall be first.
> Put on the lights when armed with binoculars!

Coming back to the balcony, the Balcony Man saw that practically all the other side was watching his side with binoculars. He could not hide his excitement and could not help being fascinated by the sight. His guests and his wife were peacefully involved in the game, and did not pay any attention to these events.

Suddenly the heart-rending cry of a woman pierced the air. The patrolman stood up and noticed the huge masses of binoculars watching them continuously. His wife looked worried and the Balcony Man's wife came near her husband. The next moment all the lights in the windows on the Watching Couple's side were lit and hundreds of people came out onto their balconies carrying binoculars and began to watch the other side.

While the Balcony Man's wife and the Police Couple were

still playing the game, they saw through their binoculars each window separately, but now, all of a sudden, they were confronted with the scene in its entirety.

For the first time they could also observe their own side. The lights were all on, and thousands of people with binoculars were spyglassing thousands of others opposite.

Without a word the Balcony Man put on the lights. Then he went to his wife and took her in his arms, but she was too fascinated to take her eyes off the scene. The patrolman did not take any notice of his wife, so enthralled was he by all that was happening around him. His wife sat in a corner of the balcony watching with stony face the stars above. Her arms were hanging limp, and the binoculars she had been using in the game were in her lap. She seemed to be the only one who was not taking part in this huge and impressive watch-in.

The patrolman stood there fully uniformed, watching the spectacular performance closely. From time to time he gasped with excitement: Incredible! Unbelievable! Inconceivable!

The Balcony Man stood there staring at the flats opposite, fascinated.

Mounted on their balconies, on their windows and on their roofs, thousands of people were watching thousands of their fellowmen in silence, like two enormous forces watching each other just before advancing. Then window would clash with window, balcony with balcony, house with house, and man with man.

From the Police Day-by-Day Report

Patrolman No. 7112 reports:

I went with my wife to visit the so-called "Watching Couple." The aim was to participate in the so-called "Game," and report of my findings regarding the complaint of the person known as "The Gentleman from the Post."

Before going to the balcony my wife and I were invited to have a small snack in the kitchen where the rules of the game were explained to us by the "Watching Couple."

After learning the rules we went to the balcony where we started to play the game. We had brought our own binoculars. (Enclosed are some diagrams and the rules of the game.)

Playing it, I found that many couples from the opposite side were also playing the game. This conclusion was based on seeing people watching our side with binoculars.

I found the game to be an amusing evening's entertainment.

At about midnight practically all the other side were on

their balconies or were popping their heads out of their windows, all or most of them armed with binoculars.

I did not find anything which was offensive or of a doubtful nature, nor a single thing during the course of the evening which could be considered illegal.

A. The police commissioner advised to submit the findings of the Game, including the rules and the diagrams, to TREED (Total Research on Essentially Everything Department) in order that the game and its effects on society might be thoroughly investigated.

The findings are to be distributed to the police within six weeks of this day.

The police commissioner has made it clear that no police interference, should it disturb the game, would be justified. "The people should be left in peace to pursue their games and pleasures after a hard day's work."

B. During the investigations an important discovery has been made.

On the side opposite to that of the "Watching Couple" in the housing development lives a dealer in binoculars who works for a certain binocular firm in town. He is known in the housing estate as "The Lonely Gentleman" as he has no family, and is often seen walking alone with a pair of binoculars round his neck.

Seeing the Watching Couple with their binoculars, the Lonely Gentleman had an idea: "I saw in it an opportunity to sell lots of binoculars to the inhabitants of the housing estate. I came up with a plan."

He stenciled letters in which he wrote "worn-out phrases of my army days" and he managed to distribute them to all the inhabitants on his side of the housing estate. (He served only six weeks in the army and was ultimately discharged for endlessly inciting violence and the killing of the enemy. In his army file it is stated that "he was creating a bad name for the army and was therefore discharged.")

Exploiting the slight panic these letters created, he "directed" people to his apartment where they could be "armed" with binoculars. In this way he managed to sell binoculars to practically everybody.

Being unable to find a law prohibiting what he claimed to be "harmless advertising of a product" we have only warned him not to use this system on any other occasion, as he might be held for creating a public disturbance.

No further steps have been taken in this direction.

In his statement the Lonely Gentleman stated that he was leaving the housing development soon, as he was moving to an "excellent villa" near the sea. He had made enough money, he stated, from selling binoculars, to be able to relax for a while and probably write his memoirs.

Then He Was Told of The Game

By lunchtime, the next day, the Gentleman Who First Discovered the Watching Couple could not stand work any longer. In a few hours time row upon row of people would confront their opponents man for man, eye to eye. The very thought made his heart go like mad.

Arriving at the housing development he went straight to the post office to meet the Gentleman from the Post and share with him the sensations of the night before.

He was told that the GP was in conference with the police. He insisted on being let in. He nearly shouted, a thing he had never done before.

In the conference room he found the GP with two patrolmen, one of whom he recognized as the one who had visited the Watching Couple. They were all laughing and in good spirits. The GP was a new man. His face was pink and he looked healthy. He was dressed most neatly. He stood up and told the GD smilingly that he was very welcome, as the subject of the conversation belonged to all.

The Gentleman Who First Discovered the Watching Couple was introduced to the two patrolmen as the Gentleman Who First Discovered the Watching Couple and was then kindly asked to take a seat.

Then he was told of The Game.

The Rules of The Game

Everybody now knew that the whole affair of the "Watching Couple" was a game and the enormous tension was gone. People were nicer as if after a war which they had managed to survive. They smiled at each other, quite relaxed, and even greeted each other.

Most of the conversation of people after work still seemed to be about the game and the "Watching Couple." From various remarks it was gathered that the most important point for most of them was that nobody really knew the rules of the game and therefore nobody dared to play it with his own family, on his own balcony.

The Gentleman from the Post was consulted, as the man who had heard the day-by-day report of the police read to him by the patrolman in the post office. But he could offer very little. He explained to people who asked him that he had hardly been able to hear the report, let alone remember the complicated rules of the game. He had been in quite a state at the time. All he could remember, he said, was that the game was played with dice and that players conceded points to each other.

In those days many people would come to the post office to try to jog the memory of the GP. This disturbed the regular work of the office considerably and, as a result, the GP was asked to take his yearly holiday immediately, in the hope that in a few weeks the game incident would be forgotten.

The Gentleman Who First Discovered the Watching Couple could not remember the rules either. He thoroughly agreed with the GP on the basic idea of the game, but differed over the awarding of points. He thought that points were not conceded but won.

The police could not be consulted on the matter for they would not, for reasons of ethics, reveal publicly the contents of their day-by-day report, not even the section covering the rules.

The only hope was to approach the Watching Couple themselves. But somehow people felt guilty toward them, so no one dared ask. The only man who probably could ever get the GD and the GP to remember even some of the rules, was the Gentleman from the Bar.

Many people pressed him to meet the two Gentlemen and find out the rules. Knowing that the two Gentlemen were themselves eager enough to remember the rules, the GB undertook the assignment. In his own initiative he invited the School Teacher, thinking the latter might be of some help, especially since the School Teacher was known to have an excellent memory. This reputation was based on the fact that year after year he remembered to tell his pupils the same stories and jokes.

That day, the GB closed his bar early and summoned the three gentlemen for the scheduled conversation.

"We are here," he said, "to try to remember the rules of the game."

"But I don't remember the rules! I've said that already a thousand times," said the Gentleman from the Post. "I wish I did."

"You say you don't remember the rules. Fine. Which part of

the rules don't you remember?"

"The specific part of the police report which speaks about the rules."

"In other words, you've merely forgotten the rules," said the School Teacher.

"That's it."

"What do you remember?"

"Well, I remember that points were conceded."

"I don't agree," said the GD. "Points were won."

"Now we're getting somewhere," said the School Teacher. "So far we know that there were points conceded or won."

"This we knew already. Points, binoculars, dice, dark and light windows. What we don't know is how you make a game out of it."

"In the police report, I remember, it was stated that the game starts with being unhappily married."

"Do you suggest that one couldn't possibly play the game if one was happily married?" asked the School Teacher.

"This sonofabitch of a Lonely Gentleman is happily unmarried and was still playing the game. What do you make of it?" said the GD.

"How do you know he played the same game? Maybe he was playing a different sort of a game?"

"Oh Christ, it never occurred to me. It's true, I didn't see the charts on his balcony."

"The charts? Which charts?" asked the School Teacher.

"Oh God, the charts! Do you remember the charts the police showed us?" exclaimed the GP.

"Right, the charts with the two tokens!" said the GD.

"Which tokens?" asked the School Teacher.

"The ones they moved on the charts."

"Go on. What else?" hopefully asked the School Teacher.

"The charts were nothing but diagrams of the buildings the

Watching Couple could see on the opposite side," said the GP.

"Splendid, then we might have the principles of the game. They move windows following the dice and win, lose, or concede points according to what they see inside the apartments," said the School Teacher. "But we don't have the most important rules of the game. We don't know what wins or what loses or how much and what is conceded. Can you remember any of the rules?"

"I can't," said the GD.

"Nor can I," said the GP.

The conference ended without noticeable results. Walking home, the GP whispered to the GD, "I wanted to tell you something. I remembered one rule."

"No!"

"Look, I remembered it but I wasn't sure that I remembered it right."

"Doesn't matter, what's the rule?"

"Seeing a Negro gives a player fifteen points and a Negro is a winner in all cases. A cop is twenty points!"

"Good God!"

"What is it?"

"We can't reveal that rule. We'll have the blacks on us. They are five points less than a cop."

"A Negro is fifteen points and a cop is twenty. But who told you that twenty points are better than fifteen?"

"Now don't give me this philosophical bullshit. Twenty is always better than fifteen. It's always more."

"There aren't any Negroes in the housing development."

"I saw a few. The point is rather what will happen when those in the city hear about it."

"Don't forget that the rule also says that a Negro is a winner in all cases."

"All the worse. We're going to have the Black Panthers coming over. They don't want to be winners in all cases, they want to be equal."

"Then we could say, for the sake of peace, that a Negro and a cop are equal, twenty points each."

"It won't work."

"Why not?"

"Because twenty points are not always equal to twenty points."

"You are wrong."

"I am not! Ask anybody!"

"I will not!"

Two days after the Gentleman from the Post went on his compulsory holiday a rumor spread round the local bar that he had told somebody before he left that he had managed to remember one of the rules of the game. Some said this rule was the key to the whole game. Some held that the rule carried dangerous implications, and therefore could not be revealed. The bar became the center of all activities concerning the game. Every evening more and more people turned out to hear and discuss the hidden mysteries. The little known was enough to arouse the imagination.

During the day the two supermarkets and the launderettes became the meeting places where the women of the housing development discussed the latest conclusions of their menfolk the night before.

All of a sudden, without knowing how, everybody knew the rule which was believed to be the one remembered by the GP: seeing a Negro gave fifteen points; a Negro was in all cases a winner. Most of the discussions were now diverted to the interpretation of the rule. No one knew the correct wording and almost everyone put forward a different point of view, guessing wildly what rule came before or after.

The first major disagreement arose over the least important

factor, the amount of points. Some said that fifteen points for a Negro was too much and that whoever had made up that number was out to embarrass Negroes. It was argued that in giving them such an excessive number of points, someone wanted to expose them (the Negroes) to public scorn.

Others said, on the other hand, that fifteen points was too few, and their reasoning was based on the same grounds as the first point of view. Everybody seemed to be worrying about the feelings of the so far unseen Negroes in the housing development. Very few thought the number fifteen was correct anyway. The second major disagreement was the interpretation of the statement that a Negro was a winner in all cases. What was meant by "in all cases"?

As someone put it: "Is a Negro better than anybody else?" People argued that if the rule said that a Negro was a winner in all cases, it obviously meant that there were others who were losers, or even winners, but certainly not in all cases. That, they said, was a precedent for deliberate and injurious discrimination and it should be stopped at once. Everybody, they said, should have equal points and equal chances.

Other people argued that it was time to grant Negroes the same kind of superiority in points so they could in due time become equals. "My best friends are Negroes," one said.

One day the police had to be called to stop a tomato fight between two ladies in one of the supermarkets.

The two ladies were unable to agree how many Negroes were in fact living in the housing development. One of the women said there were two families in all. The other claimed there were none.

Both ladies held the opinion that Negroes were victims of discrimination and should be given the right to more flats.

One of the fortunate occurrences concerning the disclosure of this rule was that the part dealing with the "twenty-point cop," was not known. But even as it was, the known part of the rule was the cause of fierce arguments.

Two big posters appeared in one of the supermarkets:

A NEGRO IS NOT BETTER THAN US!
IN GOD'S EYES ALL MEN HAVE EQUAL POINTS!

Each evening the inhabitants of the housing development would look with longing at the balcony of the Watching Couple, who continued playing their game, unconcerned. This hurt already wounded feelings and some people started to think seriously of leaving the development, even though the housing situation in the country was almost at its worst.

In the diary of a sixteen-year-old girl, there was this description:

I should like to run, to fly
To land on the balcony of the Balcony Couple.
Why won't they
Give us the right to play the game?
Why keep it to themselves?
It is mean,
It is inhuman,
It is evil.

I wrote this on the spur of the moment. It shows exactly how I feel. I know it is too romantic and sentimental. But should I run away from the truth simply because this age does not recognize the beauty of the sentimental?

Nevertheless, we are unhappy. When we had television it was more or less all right, but from the moment this game appeared, we have not watched television. You cannot watch television once you know about the game and the endless pleasures it offers. In the evening daddy either sits on the balcony watching the Watching Couple or goes to the bar to hear and discuss what is being said about the game. Mother sits with father on the balcony and when he goes to the bar she trails miserably off to bed.

I am sure there is a solution to the problem. After all, man invented the game, so why can't he invent another? Yes! That's it! Why can't we invent a new game? A game which might be more interesting than theirs. Television was also invented and it has pushed out radio. We can invent such a game that the Watching Couple will come begging on their knees for the rules of our game.

It must be possible! After all, God didn't reveal all the secrets and rules of life to His people. It took them thousands of years to find out for themselves, to invent, discover, and create them. Why can't we make another game?

Most of the people in our housing development are pretty miserable. During the big scare people had something to do. Now no one knows what to do in the evenings any more.

I wish I knew the rules of the game, I could make the people happy again.

And as if out of the blue, the housing development knew all of a sudden that the Gentleman from the Post was about to return from his holiday.

People decided to raise money to buy him a welcome-home present. Once again he was the only hope and everyone eagerly looked forward to his return.

Love

Unaware of all the discussions, sufferings, secret diaries of young girls, and longings of so many for his rules, the Balcony Man was in love.

For the last few nights the Girl on the Opposite Side was sitting on her balcony gazing at her opposite side. Wasn't she gazing at him? He was gazing at her. And absent-mindedly he continued to play the game with his wife.

It had been years since he felt this trembling of the heart. That evening, sitting on his balcony playing the game with his wife, he understood, probably for the first time, that this was his life. That no other form of life existed and that his life meant sitting with his wife on the balcony each evening and loving the Girl on the Opposite Side. The moment he realized that, he felt relieved and even happy.

It was a bright night. His binoculars were resting on her eyes, her big glowing eyes. The eyes of Enid. Enid the fair, who has made his heart tremble, beat-tremble each evening.

It was Enid he was in love with. Enid watched him and he watched her. Enid was a dream fulfilled through his eyes.

Watching her, he could feel all his being streaming along their sight-beams.

He smelled her through his eyes, he tasted her, he touched her, he cuddled her.

He stroked her hair, he laughed with her. All through his eyes. Enid was the luckiest girl to have him, and he was the luckiest man to have her.

He had never met her. He did not even know her name. He had invented Enid for her. It was a name good as any other.

He went to the kitchen to make some coffee. Through the kitchen window he saw Enid going to her kitchen too. He knew exactly what her kitchen looked like. It was a replica of his. He knew where her hand went for the coffee, to light the gas, to get out the cup, the spoon, the tray. He knew where Enid slept, how the bed was arranged and which wall it faced. He knew where she put her lovely head, where the bedroom window was and what she saw through it. He even knew what colors Enid saw before she closed her eyes. He could not see her bedroom because its window faced the other side of the block. But he knew. It was exactly the same as his and a thousand other flats.

Knowing all this about Enid made him endlessly happy. After all, the memory of a love, when it loses its actuality, always turns to colors, shapes, sounds, and smells. He even knew the sound her bedroom door made when she closed it. He knew her shower and knew its sound. The shower which rained its water on her erect white body.

When he walked into his flat, he walked into her flat. When he wanted to switch on the lights, he went where Enid went. They lived the same life in their separate flats in their separate buildings.

When she watched his flat she found her flat in his, as he found his when he watched hers. He even knew the things he could not see from his balcony. He did not guess at them, he knew them.

He went back to the balcony where his wife was waiting for him. He brought her coffee and joined the game again. Enid had switched off the lights and the light in the small window of the bathroom was on. He got up and went to the bathroom, wishing not only to experience exactly what Enid experienced, but also to experience it at the same time. The sound of the shower has a special music when you know that at the same moment, somewhere, your girl, whom you love, is hearing the same sounds, feeling the same water, and thinking the same thoughts. He opened the shower and put his hand under the water. Time is an important factor in such a love. It wouldn't be the same to hear the water, even if the sound was the same, if Enid were not hearing it at the same time. Now Enid and he were bound by the voice of the water, by the sight of the water, by the feel of the water.

His wife came to see what the hell he was doing in the bathroom and why he had turned on the shower. They laughed, and he went back to the balcony. Enid was in bed now. Everything was dark. They were parted. He wanted to lie in bed in the same place where Enid lay. To put his head where Enid put hers. To be there when she was there. Time was passing quickly. They were still on the balcony. Some people on the opposite side were going to their beds, others stayed on. Enid was asleep by now. He had lost the thread which was their togetherness. The next day was to be another night.

Before going to bed he took a shower. It was not the same. The voice of its waters was quite different now from when Enid took her shower. It spoke of different things. He went to bed. His wife came too. They discussed the game a little and gossiped a bit, and laughed. They put off the light. They went into one another's arms. They slept.

Why Does James Joyce Win The Game?

Next day, coming back from the city, the Balcony Man did not go straight home. He wanted to be alone and work things out. He had the feeling that some people from the housing development knew about his love for Enid. The thought that they were participating in his most intimate moments made him feel closer to them.

Only a few hours before the arrival of the GP, the Balcony Man walked into the bar and calmly ordered a beer. The surprise was so great that no one dared move or say a word. The Gentleman from the Bar was stunned and it took him some time to recover and serve the beer to his very special customer. As it was still early evening only a few people were present, but they were the first of many who would have come later to attend the welcome-home party for the return of the Gentleman from the Post.

Cutting short his dinner, the GD ran to the bar. Also headed toward the bar was the School Teacher, who was trying hard to keep in step with his beautiful and attractive teenage daughter.

The Balcony Man was sitting in a corner drinking his beer. He knew that his game had caused a certain panic in the housing development and that people were probably annoyed with him. But now that everybody knew it was only a game, he felt they had no reason to be annoyed. Still he was uncertain as to their possible reaction.

The moment the GD followed by the School Teacher and his daughter entered the bar, the tension mounted considerably. He and she sat at separate tables without giving a sign that they knew each other. They only nodded to the GB, who in turn nodded back.

After a short while the GB winked at the School Teacher and at the GD. They winked back, and there followed a lot of winking between them.

By now the bar was quite crowded. Nobody talked except for a few who were whispering to each other.

The GD went to the GB who stood behind the bar and whispered, "Maybe he would like to have some money for the rules?"

"You mean to buy them from him?"

"Why not?"

"It might be a good idea. How much should we offer?"

"I don't know. We could pass a piece of paper around and ask each person the amount he thinks should be offered."

"And we'll all share the expenses."

In whispers they passed the word. The piece of paper was moved around until it reached the School Teacher's daughter who did not understand the idea. Seeing all sorts of numbers written on it, thinking they might be numbers of points, somehow connected with the game or a delicate hint for the Balcony Man, she passed the piece of paper to him. Everybody held his breath. The Balcony Man looked at the people, blushed, stood up, handed the paper to the GB, and said apologetically: "Excuse me, but I don't know the rules."

Everybody gasped.

"You don't know the rules?" asked the GB astonished. "How did you play then?"

"I didn't, but I don't mind joining."

The GB and the GD stared at him flabbergasted. The teenage daughter of the School Teacher cried in despair, "But you've invented the game!"

"You mean my game?"

"Yes."

"Oh."

"Everybody here wants to know the rules!"

"Yes," cried a few people.

"You mean you want to play the game?"

"We'd like to, if you've nothing against it."

"On the contrary. Be my guests."

"You'll tell us the rules?"

"No problems, and don't forget to tell me later the rules of your game."

"Which game?"

"The game with the numbers on the piece of paper."

The chairs were arranged round the Balcony Man. The GD whispered to the GB in passing, "We better tell him about the numbers on the piece of paper."

"Nonsense, if we can get them free, why should we pay for them?"

By now everybody was sitting round the Balcony Man. The School Teacher agreed to write down the rules. Explaining the rules of the game, the Balcony Man was interrupted from time to time by various questions.

"Who is James Joyce, and why does he win the game?"

"Does he live in the housing development?"

"Could one see a real sexual intercourse?"

"What is the difference between fiction and nonfiction—and which of it is drama or poetry?"

"Is *Screw* a mechanical manual?"

(The School Teacher's daughter smiled.)

"Why is *Good Housekeeping* only one point less than *Screw?*"

"What happens if one sees something which is not mentioned in the rules?"

(They decided then and there to have five points win for things not mentioned in the original rules.)

"Can anybody add to the rules?"

"Is there anybody who owns the game?"

Each question was answered carefully by the Balcony Man. Finishing his detailed description of the game, he drew some diagrams to illustrate and explain the moves of the tokens.

Although he took some persuading the Headmaster was fetched in order to obtain his permission to use the school stenciling machine at that hour of the night.

In a few hours a set of the rules had been stenciled, duplicated, and delivered to each family. By midnight everyone of the thousands of people on the housing development knew the entire pattern of the game.

Late that night, after stenciled rules had been delivered to the various flats, the Gentleman from the Post was found sitting near the closed door of the bar. He was utterly miserable. At first he did not want to speak to anybody. Somewhat later when the GB told him that it was thanks to him that the Balcony Man agreed to reveal the game's rules, he tried to stand up but failed. Then he broke down and started to sob.

From the few words he managed to say it was clear that two days before his return he had been notified about the party the GB and others were giving for him. Arriving home he had hurried to change and put on his best suit. Coming to the bar where the party was to take place he found it dark and closed. At first he thought it was a kind of joke, and that, all of a sudden, people would spring on him from all sides to bring him into the party; but it did not happen. Then he sat down near the bar entrance and fell asleep.

He was taken home and the GD sat up with him late into the night.

Back home the Balcony Man's wife was angry. "You shouldn't have told them the rules," she said.

"But why?"

"Because if everybody starts playing the game then there is no longer a game!"

"What do you mean by 'everybody starts playing the game?'"

"Everybody starts watching the apartments on the opposite side."

"Does life stop?" asked the Balcony Man.

"Life goes on. So what?"

"Then the game goes on too."

"You'll be damned surprised to find out what a small part life plays in the lives of most people!" said the Balcony Man's wife.

"Wasn't it the same before I told them the rules? People ate, quarreled, watched TV, went to their bathroom, undressed, made love, if ever. By the way, 99 per cent go to sleep with their pajamas on, have you noticed it? Nevertheless, even if they'll all play the game, they'll go on doing the same things as before."

"They'll restrain themselves."

"There will be many more people who'd do much more of everything knowing they're being watched."

"For kicks?"

"Also, but mainly because in their adult life very few are ever being watched. At least not with sympathy."

"People will see the same things," said the Balcony Man's wife.

"The same things?" wondered the Balcony Man thinking of

Enid.

It was late. Enid could not be there. Just to make sure, he went to the balcony. She was there! Waiting. He lifted the binoculars to his eyes. Enid. She was so young and so beautiful and she was waiting for him. Hours, days, years did not count any longer. Love without speech, love without touch, without smell, without a thousand little things—but blooming, nevertheless. She looked like a school girl, shy, somewhat embarrassed and half smiling. Her breasts were erect, and sharply pointed toward him, trying to burst and detach themselves in amorous flight to him.

Now that he had told them the rules would he lose Enid to them?

"I'll join you in a minute," he called to his wife who was already lying in bed. "What a situation to be in," he thought.

Points

Life took on a new form in the housing development. In a matter of days the rules of the game had been studied and discussed within each family, and were finally an integral part of everyone's life.

The Big Game had started.

People in the area spoke of nothing else. Everyone everywhere exchanged views on the game and its big advantages over television and other popular entertainments.

Numerous worlds, shut to strangers before, opened up and were visited by hundreds of pairs of binoculars. Just a few days after the evening they had learned the rules, many families and singles were out on their balconies playing the game.

With each passing evening more and more people would forsake their TV and join the cult of the gameplayers. Everybody who wanted to watch, watched, those who wanted to be watched, were watched, and people who did not play the game for one reason or another would rarely close their blinds.

Two days after the rules of the game were disclosed by the Balcony Man, the School Teacher told his pupils that though the game was an enthralling pastime and he was playing it with great pleasure, he could not agree fully with its rules.

In a matter of hours the entire development knew of the dissenting opinions of the School Teacher. No one knew exactly what his opinion was, but as far as could be gathered from the boys and girls, the School Teacher had changed some of the rules and was playing the game in his own way.

At the request of the parents, the GB together with the GP went to the School Teacher to ask him to explain his views.

Meeting them for an afternoon tea party, the School Teacher pointed out that he had not actually changed all the rules of the game, which he confessed to admiring, but only some of them, especially those connected with the amount of points won or lost.

He did not want to disclose his scale of points, but he revealed that he had consulted his family and that the scale of points was connected to his own scale of values.

The GP and the GB could not accept such vagueness and pressed for clear answers.

"You said that your scale of points was connected to your scale of values," asked the GP. "What does that mean precisely?"

"It means that values and points are related," said the School Teacher.

"This really goes over my head," said the GB. "Why on earth can't you tell us your rules?"

"The Balcony Man gave his," said the GP. "You can give yours."

"His rules were not connected with values. My rules are my life!" declared the School Teacher.

"Shall we slow down a bit? Please!" said the GB. "I don't get the whole goddamn thing. Is this one of your values not to tell your rules?"

"Yes, the value of privacy."

"Goddamn it, what do you mean by value of privacy? Every night you are touring the apartments of others, aren't you?"

"But that's their privacy not mine."

"What happens when they watch your apartment?

"That's O.K. too. We exchange privacies. The value of privacy doesn't mean not to let people into your apartment, but rather to let those you have chosen."

"So if it's only a matter of choice, this value of privacy, you could choose to tell us the rules of the game," said the GP.

"I certainly could. I choose not to."

"But give us only an example, so we have something to tell. Just give us an example . . ."

"O.K.," said the School Teacher, "I'll give you an example. Take the rule which says that seeing a kissing couple wins seven points. This rule is morally unacceptable. I argued with my wife about it and then with my daughter. I did convince them at last. We have changed this rule. Seeing a kissing couple loses five points now."

"Why the hell must a couple who kisses lose?" asked the GB amazed.

Looking at the GB with pity the School Teacher said, "The rule as it stood encouraged couples to actually expose their intimate and private affairs and might have created havoc with the values of family life. It would be a disaster! It would encourage kissing."

"Is that right?"

"And not only that gentlemen, but it would be the end of family life."

"God Almighty!"

"Another example of my changes," continued the School Teacher, "and with which my wife and my daughter totally agreed, was that seeing a grown-up person reading a book used to be winning three points. We have changed it. Now it wins twenty-one points. I had to manifest the importance of book reading!"

"Then what about seeing a couple having a Babunka?" asked the GB.

"Having what?"

"Babunka."

"What for Christ sake is a Babunka?" asked the School Teacher.

"Well, you know, a couple is making it . . ."

"In what language is that other word?" panicked the School Teacher.

"In Malayalam, the language of Malabar. I've heard it from a sailor," said the GB. "I kind of like the word, don't you?"

"It's not bad," said the GP.

"It's outrageous," said the School Teacher.

"Well, anyhow how many points?"

"No comment."

"What do you mean no comment? Babunka is not a four-letter word!"

"The game is becoming a beautiful family affair. I don't want to spoil it by referring to such an anti-family act. I told you the principle of the changes I made. Let me say only that the rules must correspond with the values of the family members. Change, to my opinion, is always desirable," ended the School Teacher. "Farewell."

Points Fever

As soon as these changes were known, people became infected by what came to be known as "Points Fever."

Not only did each family try to change the scale of points, according to their different beliefs and moral systems, but many people started to think in terms of points in their daily life. Even teenage slang reflected this interest. Teenagers evaluated everything in terms of points: "A seven-point girl," "a three-point dinner," "twenty-point tits," and so on.

Even if the original scale of points matched their own temperament, people would change at least something in order to conform to the revolutionary milieu they were now living in, and also to get involved emotionally with Points Fever.

The GD felt at first uneasy about changing the original rules. It was widely known that it was he who had first discovered the Watching Couple and that made him feel the custodian of them and of everything they had established.

That evening he invited the Gentleman from the Post and one of the Supermarket Ladies to join him and his wife in their game.

When the GP and his Supermarket Lady discovered that the GD and his wife were playing the game with the original rules of the Balcony Man they started reproaching them for not having changed them.

"Everybody has his own personal opinions about things and has to live up to them," said the GP. "We don't want our society to turn into a society where one rule governs everybody. Therefore everybody should change the rules according to his own beliefs and values. We should keep our individuality as long as we can!"

"Everybody's changing the rules?" The GD's wife was shocked. "We've got to change them at once!"

"What the hell!" said the GD. "You said something about the goddamn rule governing our goddamn society. What is it if not one rule?"

"When everybody has changed the rules every individual will have a different set of rules."

"If everybody should change the rules, it's still one rule which governs everybody: 'Everybody should change the rules.'"

"But this is not a rule, it's a certain stage everybody should go through in order to come to the point where there is no one rule which governs everybody."

"Bullshit. That's the second rule you're making which again applies to everybody: 'Everybody should go through a certain stage in order to come to whatever the hell you said.'"

"It starts with everybody making the same steps, in order to reach later their freedom and individuality."

"Now that everybody's changing the rules, and everybody's making the same steps, I'm the only one left who's not changing the rules and who's not making the same steps," said the GD. "My rules are already different from anybody's. I'm probably the only one who still plays with the old rules!"

"Yes, but your rules are a remnant of the past. These rules are not yours. You don't believe in them. Somebody else has invented them for you."

"That's right, but I still like them."

"Do you believe, for instance, that James Joyce should win the game?"

"I don't mind."

"You don't mind because you don't even know who James Joyce is."

"Of course, I know. I heard about him in the bar. He was a writer."

"Good. But you haven't read anything by him."

"No."

"Then why should he win the game. Maybe he was a lousy writer?"

"No doubt about it, but what's it to do with the game? It's only a game, isn't it?"

"But which you play with real people and the rules apply to what these people do."

"So what?"

"Your points must go according to your moral code. The School Teacher didn't believe that kissing in public is right, so he made kissing a loser."

"The School Teacher is crazy."

"Sure, but at least he believes in something."

"Isn't it better not to believe in anything than to believe in something which is silly?"

"So you don't believe in anything, is that it?"

"I do. I believe in playing the game and in just being happy."

But after a considerable amount of pressure had been put on the GD, he decided to give in and make some changes to the rules. After all, one did not live alone! Sometimes one had to give in to the demands of society, even if personally one thought otherwise.

Because he was going to change the rules without really being convinced of the necessity of doing so, he could not regard each rule individually but wanted to find something which would make everyone who heard about his changes gasp with excitement. Although everyone in the housing development was keeping his changes secret because revealing them would mean more or less exposing one's own character to the public, everybody knew of the changes each family had made, or was planning to make.

He thought that there would be no difficulty in letting people know of his changes.

After talking with his wife about it, he changed the scale of points so that what was originally a winner became a loser and the losers became winners. In that way, everything unusual now lost points and everything usual won. This was diametrically opposed to the original rules, and was obviously much more drastic than anything anybody else in the housing development would dream of.

As he had predicted, the entire development immediately knew that the GD had changed the original rules in a most radical way. Immediately after that everybody knew that the change he had made was a complete reversal of the original. Many families who had changed the rules, blindly following the example of the School Teacher, found themselves in a difficult position. More and more people started to follow the new rules of the GD until they grew to be a large Radical Group in the housing development. The GD once more became a popular figure.

A few nights after he had changed the rules, his wife, having lost a large number of points and nearly the game, in a sudden outburst started to scream at him hysterically. She said he was a crook, a liar, and a cheat. She shouted that before he had changed the rules, she'd lost points for seeing a television set, and now, after the radical change, she was still losing points for television sets. She shouted that he was cheating everybody and that he hadn't actually changed anything.

"How is it possible," she shrieked, "that before you altered the rules, TV sets always made me lose points, and now you have changed the rules, these blasted TV sets still make me lose points?"

The GD could see that she was right but he could not explain how it was possible. He did not understand it either. Trying to calm her down, he promised to think about it and correct the error. "I want to win when I see a television set," she shouted and stormed off to her room. Thinking about it the GD realized that since people had started playing the game they had stopped watching television in the evenings. The original rules were based on the everyday life of the housing development. He had turned them upside down. But reality had also been turned upside down. Thus he achieved the same result as if the game had been played with the original rules. Actually he had not changed anything.

As no one was watching television now and most of the TV sets in the area were permanently off, the only way to make his wife win points from a television set was, absurd as it seemed, go back to the original rule. That is to say a television off wins. That way his wife could win her points. That was the only way.

Thinking further, he found many other queer things, as a result of his changes. If only they knew that the "Radical Changes" I pretended to make have not changed anything! he thought. And now, to satisfy his wife, he had to change the rules back to the original, so she could win points by seeing a television off.

No one knew that the GD had created a "Points Disaster," but he was sure someone would notice it soon.

The Window Society

At this point the first serious difficulty, involving many families, arose in the housing development. The problem concerned people who could see very few windows from their balconies. That obviously made it quite difficult for them to play the game, especially with its existing rules.

These families tried hard to find a solution for their unfortunate situation. They created an exclusive club, where they could meet and freely discuss their problem. It was named "The Window Society."

The only qualification required for membership of the Window Society was being unable to see more than twenty-five windows from one's own balcony. The Window Society had its daily meetings every evening in one of its member's flats. As they could find no viable solution in the foreseeable future, these meetings turned into social gatherings.

Everyone in the housing development knew who belonged to the Window Society and looked down upon them.

Funnily enough, the flats which overlooked the fewest buildings and windows were the most expensive ones in the housing development. This is why the Window Society consisted only of well-to-do people who held quite important positions in the city.

The scornful remarks made by the Game People about the Window Society as "being the wealthiest among the residents of the housing development," "all their wealth could not help them play the game," soon became scandalous. This was too much for the Window Society. Its chairman, known as the Window Gentleman, came out with a well-prepared declaration, denouncing all the slanderous gossip. He ended his statement with the following touching tale:

"Looking out of our windows at the green landscape, fringed by mountains and dotted with lakes—is no longer a pleasure. The valleys and slopes with their narrow paths winding and curling until they vanish away behind the hills—is nobody's joy. The game with its human landscapes and real life is all we long for."

After this pathetic plea, the superior attitude of the Game People toward the Window Society changed into one of pity and sympathy. The Game People started to do their very best to cheer up the Window Society and tried to find ways of compensating them for their lost pleasure.

The solution was found by the Window Gentleman. He explained that there were around fifty families in the Window Society, apart from a few who had not become members for one reason or another. On average each one of the Window Families could see from fifteen to twenty windows. This meant that all of them together could see between seven hundred fifty to one thousand windows in all. "Why not play together?" the Window Gentleman exclaimed.

It was true that the Watching Couple, for example, had thousands of windows in their possession, but there were families who didn't have more than three or four hundred windows and they could still play the game quite successfully.

"If we join forces and have trust in each other we can play the game like everybody else," the Window Gentleman told his listeners.

His actual plan was to divide the Window Society into two groups for the purposes of the game. Each group would then be able to see from their balconies approximately four hundred fifty windows with which they could play. The two groups would play one against the other.

It would have to be decided which would be the starting window for each group, the finishing window, and the route.

The groups would take turns to throw the dice, and within the groups each family would throw the dice in alphabetical order. The description of what was to be seen inside a certain flat by one family would be communicated to the rest by telephone. The game would be won once a week and the group leader would be changed every week. The same evening the Window Gentleman declared that those who "might think that this version of the game would tempt players to describe over the phone things they had never seen, in order to influence the results of the game, should not forget that the Window Society was based on total confidence."

The Window Gentleman made a plea to the School Teacher begging him to let the Window Society use his set of rules, as he considered the School Teacher to be of great integrity and honor. The School Teacher answered that if the Window Society as a body would approach him in connection with the rules he would seriously consider the matter.

On the spot every one of the members signed a petition which was sent to the School Teacher. The same evening he agreed to let the Window Society have his rules. They became known throughout the housing development, as if in a fraction of a minute.

It will be of some interest here to set out part of the School

Teacher's scale of points and compare it with that of the Watching Couple.

THE WATCHING COUPLE

	To Win	*To Lose*
A Negro	15	
Kissing couple	7	
Couple fighting		9
Sexual intercourse	32	
Naked woman	6	
Cleaning flat		7
Reading James Joyce	Wins the game	
Screw	56	
Half-naked man		73

THE SCHOOL TEACHER

	To Win	*To Lose*
Grandma telling story to children	15	
Kissing couple		5
Dad leaves Mum alone		99
Mother cooking for family	32	
Dad talking to his children	6	
Cleaning flat	7	
Reading New Testament	Wins the game	
Charlotte's Web	57	
Boy with long hair		73

In a matter of days the two groups of the Window Society started to play the game against each other, both adopting the rules of the School Teacher.

The housing development showed great interest in the Window Society, firstly because of the new set of rules, unknown till then, and secondly because it introduced a new mode of playing the game, in the sense that each family was no longer playing alone, but several families joined forces and created two united blocks playing one against the other. Having solved their problem the Window Society retired itself. Its members, like everybody else in the housing development, now spent every evening sitting on their balconies, playing the game.

The Corner People and the Icebox Club

Now that their interest and attention were no longer taken up by the Window Society, the Game People began to notice that a few families in the housing development were not playing the game. Although only a few, these families were divided into two major groups.

The first consisted mainly of artists, painters, writers, and actors who just did not find the game interesting enough to play. They did not even mind being squares in other people's games, nor did they mind being watched and utilized. They became known as the Corner People and were treated by the Game People with some understanding.

The other group of non-playing families was larger, and consisted of people who besides not being in the least attracted to the game were also annoyed by the fact that merely by existing and moving around their own flats they were helping others to play the game. They could not stand the idea of becoming objects in somebody else's game, knowing that whatever they did in their own homes added or subtracted points for someone else. Being conscious of this fact, they became aggressive toward the game and kept trying to find some way of disrupting it and annoying its players. This group became known as the Icebox Club.

Among the Icebox Club there was a man, fat and with a long beard, who lived alone and became known in the housing development as the Light Gentleman. The reason for such a name was that every evening he sat in the corner of his room and kept switching the lights on and off.

On one occasion he explained that by so doing he was manifesting his personal protest against only existing in somebody else's game. To the Icebox Club's protest that, contrary to his wish, his light-show simply gave the game more possibilities and made it more fascinating, he answered that one should register one's own protest according to one's own vision, regardless of the consequences, whatever they might be. In this way the fat Light Gentleman became an alien within his own group.

The rest of the Icebox Club also tried to show their personal disapproval of the game and actually found a way of disrupting it. One of these families came up with a concrete suggestion. "Seeing someone opposite cleaning his house makes a player lose seven points. Someone cleaning his windows loses a player six points. Therefore each of our people should start cleaning their flats and windows every evening. Apart from demonstrating our disgust with the game, this would also make people lose points and would consequently turn them against it." The idea was considered and finally put into operation.

By now, the game was being played according to three major sets of rules:

A. The Original (of the Watching Couple).
B. The Radical Change (of the GD).
C. The School Teacher's Rules.

Most of the players adopted the "B" and "C" sets of rules. The family who suggested annoying the Game People by cleaning flats and windows in the evenings did not take these facts into consideration. They based their plan of attack on the original rules of the Watching Couple, forgetting that in the two other sets of rules flat-cleaning and window-cleaning were winners.

Thus a rather strange situation arose. The Ladies and Gentlemen from the Icebox Club were seen each evening cleaning their flats for hours, while most of the players enjoyed the increased chances of winning a considerable number of points.

The excitement the Game People derived from the game grew with each passing evening. The game lent them endless opportunities of discovering new things and of getting emotionally involved with many of the affairs of the other families. The two non-playing groups, the Corner People and the Icebox Club, were totally ignored and forgotten.

Peeping Tom

Without much ado and somehow naturally, the GD, the GP, and the GB became the unofficial committee of the game. Any of the residents of the housing development who had a question, a complaint, or a suggestion approached one of the three gentlemen.

One of the repeated complaints communicated to the committee, mainly by the female participants in the game, was what they called the appearance of the Peeping Tom. A few women complained of being peeped at. The three gentlemen were in a state of perplexity. How was it possible for anyone to be a Peeping Tom in a society which was based on peeping?

One of the complaining women said that she had seen a man on the opposite side who, "although he pretends to play the game, is a Peeping Tom." But when another woman called the GB and told him: "Yesterday I spotted a Peeping Tom! He watched me with binoculars!" he got quite irritated. "Wait a minute," he shouted, "what the hell do you mean by 'he watched me with binoculars?' Everybody's watching with binoculars. That's the game. You must be crazy!"

"I'm not," she cried. "I've spotted a Peeping Tom."

"You don't mean to say that everyone around here is a Peeping Tom, do you?"

"God forbid no, but he is."

"How do you know?"

"I feel it."

Following other similar calls, the three gentlemen, though unwillingly, decided to visit at least two of the "accused" men.

The GP had some difficulties in explaining to the first man they visited what he had been accused of: "Well, it's difficult to explain . . . a certain woman complained that . . . well . . . that you watch her with . . . binoculars . . ."

"What?" shouted the man. "You are crazy! Out! I'll call the police! Out! Help!"

"Please take it easy," said the GB.

"What do you mean I'm watching her with binoculars? Of course I'm watching her with binoculars! Everybody's watching with binoculars!"

"But do you watch in order to play the game or do you play the game in order to watch?" asked the GP.

"You are crazy! I refuse to answer anything of that kind before I get in touch with my therapist. This is my constitutional right! I'm not conscious of any breach of law. I play the game! And like everybody else I watch, and like everybody else I like it! Out!"

The three gentlemen decided to change their attitude and play it more straight. This demanded a certain amount of courage but they were confident. They entered the second man's apartment and the GB declared at once: "I am sorry to say, but you have been accused by a certain woman who lives on the other side of being a Peeping Tom!"

The man remained silent. Sitting down he said pathetically: "Yes, I am."

"What?" cried the three gentlemen.

"I knew that one day I'd be caught again," said the man sadly. "I've no place on this earth. I'll have to do something about it."

"Please, don't get depressed," pleaded the GP. "Everything will be all right. Don't worry."

"Don't worry? How am I to go on living when I am a Peeping Tom? And, getting caught."

"Please, don't get so upset," said the GD. "After all you don't do anything different from anybody else. Like them, you just watch."

"Is that what you think?" hopefully asked the man.

"Well, maybe you enjoy it more, but basically you are not breaking any law. You are now a part of the majority."

"Do you mean that I was in the minority before? Is that what you're saying?"

"Well, you were a kind of a pioneer in the field."

"Really?"

"Sort of."

"Oh God. I should have committed suicide. I detest weirdos!"

"Now that the accepted moral code compliments your character, there is nothing to worry about."

"I'll kill myself. Without delay. Now!" cried the man.

The three gentlemen got hold of him.

"Now listen well, buddy," said the GB. "To be a Peeping Tom in our housing development now is only an advantage! If you weren't one you had to kill yourself. But now? It is legalized, authorized, allowed and even encouraged. And you've got all that know-how."

"Well, in that case," said the Peeping Tom, "I have changed my mind. I'll live with it."

The GD, GP, and GB were shocked and confused when they left the Peeping Tom. Never had they thought of defending such an act. But they sensed they were right. In this case as in the case of the TV rule and the GD's wife, reality had changed. And as in the case of the TV rule, people had to confront the new reality, with its new values. If Peeping Tomism had been rare and therefore punishable, the changing reality had made Peeping Tomism commonplace and the rules had to be changed. Peeping Tomism became an unpunishable act. In fact, Peeping Tomism had at last come into its own.

The Sunnyside and the Shadowside

In the most natural way, each side of the huge housing development became more united and the families living on the same side became more attached to each other. Without any visible attempt and without a preliminary warning the housing development found itself divided into two factions. Due to the fact that they were situated at quite different angles to the sun, the two sides became known as The Sunnyside and The Shadowside.

It was one of those full-moon nights when a family playing on the Shadowside spotted a teenage boy they had never seen before, visiting the School Teacher's family. It was immediately understood that he had come to visit their beautiful teenage daughter. Before the School Teacher left his balcony to re-enter the flat, a member of one of the playing families opposite collected seven points (they were playing with the original rules) when he landed on the corridor window, where he saw the youngsters kiss in haste before the father arrived.

The School Teacher and the boy, who looked quite embarrassed, had a long argument in the corridor. By now almost everybody on the Shadowside knew about it. Those who could see it through their own binoculars went on playing the game, with one eye on the teenagers and their problems. At the same time some other events were taking place in other flats too, so one had to be wide awake to all that life was perpetually offering. Those who could not see the teenagers could witness other incidents of interest. The telephone always helped to keep people informed of the latest developments.

The School Teacher eventually got quite angry. His daughter started to cry and the boy was seen leaving. At that moment many on the Shadowside felt guilty and annoyed with the School Teacher, who reappeared on his balcony to continue playing the game with his wife. But the next moment, as one of the families who could see the teenager's kitchen window reported by telephone that the girl was climbing down the drainpipe straight into her lover's arms, everybody was laughing heartily.

Late in the evening the teenage daughter came back home, climbed up the pipe, and appeared quite innocently on the balcony where her parents, blissfully unaware of what was going on, were still playing their game.

Naturally, that caused stormy debates among the people. Some held the opinion, contrary to others, that kissing is immoral. Others said that fathers should keep out of their daughters' business, contrary to others who claimed just the opposite. Some said that the beautiful daughter was right in doing what she did; others said it was irresponsible. It seemed that everybody had very clear views on everything. But every night some of the families on the Shadowside won or lost points because of the Kissing Couple. It all depended on what set of rules one was using to play the game.

The Sunnyside turned out to be a happy side for the male inhabitants of the housing development. For one reason. A few evenings a week most of the people of the Sunnyside would see in one of the flats on the Shadowside a young girl of about sixteen years of age, dressed in a fashionable mini-see-thru nightgown, moving about in her room in a kind of a bizarre motion, talking to someone on the phone, while her parents, unaware of anything, were out on their balcony enthusiastically playing the game. Some thought that she was dancing, others speculated that she indulged in modern Yoga exercises. It seemed strange that she did it while holding the telephone receiver pressed to her ear.

By now people were used to seeing all kinds of strange behavior on the opposite side, so that even the most conservative among them did not revolt against such an act. To be sure, most of the men enjoyed it and even started to share their excitement with their wives.

No one from the Sunnyside knew that people from the Shadowside saw more or less the same performance. But in their case it was performed by a man. He was about thirty-five years old and quite handsome. Though he would not be dressed transparently, he would perform sort of a dance while holding the telephone receiver pressed to his ear.

No one in the housing development could see both the young girl and the man, and so no one could know the secret.

It started with a short casual meeting between the thirty-five-year-old man and the sixteen-year-old girl, in one of the supermarkets in the housing development.

That same evening the young girl was sitting tentatively on her balcony, playing the game with her parents. The moment her man stood up to go to the phone she went into her room. The phone did not ring more than one second before she picked it up.

"It's me," whispered the man.

"I know," she whispered.

"Do you know I love you?" asked the man shyly.

"Yes," said the girl.

"Since when did you know it?"

"You remember the evening, about two weeks ago, when you had a couple of friends at your place. And you went to the balcony every few minutes to look at me?"

"So you were looking at me too."

"Yes."

"You love me?"

"Yes."

"Do you think we could meet one day?"

"I don't see how we can. During the day you work and I am at school. In the evening I must be here."

"But you could find a way if you really wanted to."

"Don't you believe I want to be with you?"

"Of course I do."

"Don't you believe I have never been with any man before?"

"I do."

"I am only sixteen you know. And not from the city."

"Yes but love is not only words."

"I agree."

"I want to make love to you."

"So do I."

"So?" asked the man in expectation.

"Shall we try?" exclaimed the girl.

"What do you mean?"

"Just that."

"Just what?"

"I mean through the phone."

"You mean to make love through the telephone?" the man asked shocked.

"I've dreamt I'll do it with you one day."

"How?"

"I'll tell you what I do to you and you'll tell me what you do to me."

"So?"

"Then you'll do to yourself what I say I do to you and I'll do to myself what you say you do to me. We also can watch each other."

"But all our side, thousands of people, will see you!" cried the man.

"So what? As long as it's not my father or somebody from our side, I don't care."

"All your side will see me!"

"But nobody will be able to see both of us at the same time. So we can make love without being disturbed."

"Oh, hell. How does one start making love like this?"

"Just give me a kiss."

"O.K."

"No. You can't say O.K. You have to say what do you do to me."

"I wish I could hold your breasts."

"They are yours."

"They are beautiful."

"They are hard. Feel? Go on, please tell me more. Please."

"I am taking your bra away."

"No."

"What's the matter?"

"I never wear a bra."

"Hell."

"You're disappointed?"

"It would have been fun."

"Take me. Please touch me. I want you. Please."

"You haven't even once said what you are doing to me. Nobody's touching ME!"

"I am."

"I thought you should tell me first what you are doing to me. It was your idea to make love through the telephone," complained the man.

"I know. I thought I could say anything."

"Can't you?"

"I'll try. I don't know all the names though."

"You can invent them; it might work."

"I kiss your binoculars!"

"What the hell does that stand for?"

"It stands for that, I don't know the name of it."

"Why binoculars?"

"I don't know really. I suppose, like binoculars, that is a sort of extension of oneself."

"Damn it. Find better metaphors. Make love to me. Speak!"

The man, holding the telephone receiver with one hand and the binoculars with the other, was now fully excited by the sight of her. He tried not to look at her parents, who were going on with the game undisturbed.

The men on the Sunnyside also enjoyed the sight. Women felt pity for the girl's parents. On the other hand women on the Shadowside enjoyed the man, but the men on that side pitied him for his loneliness.

The young girl did not have any trouble in retiring to her room in the middle of the game. The moment he would see the man on the opposite side retiring to his room, knowing full well what would follow, her father would always instruct his daughter to go to her room. He had quite a moralistic view on education. He thought that seeing such a man, who was most probably crazy, would have a damaging effect on his daughter. As she never objected to her father's proposition to retire to her own room, he felt that his endless efforts regarding his daughter's upbringing were bearing satisfying results.

But the moment it became known and a moral scandal

started to build up, the shocked father decided to leave the housing development at once. But after some consultations he agreed to have his daughter marry her Telephone Man, rather than leave the game.

The Telephone Couple hastily married to the satisfaction of both sides of the housing development.

Because of such incidents, people from one side of the housing development got to know each other and wherever they met they exchanged views on things they commonly saw on the other side. They had much to talk about! And much in common.

Confusion

Three months had passed since the Balcony Man first appeared on his balcony to discover the game.

Now that the sides were more or less established, it became inevitable that he would be asked to head the committee on his side, the Sunnyside.

One evening when the Balcony Man was waiting for the appearance of Enid on her balcony, three people from his side came to see him. At that moment Enid appeared on her balcony. The Balcony Man was at a loss. Silently parting from Enid he went to meet his guests. The three neighbors began by announcing that the opposite side, the Shadowside, was organizing itself. "We must do the same," they said. They had very strange arguments. They said that because "we (our Sunnyside) can see them (their Shadowside), but cannot see our own side, it is only natural for us to become more friendly with the people we cannot see and whose lives we cannot know." That was why the Sunnyside, so they said, should keep close together. "We have common interests," they said. "We see the same things. And what's more," they continued, "we cannot watch each other," they concluded in triumph.

They wanted him to head the committee which was to organize his side. They said he was one of the most intelligent people living on the Sunnyside. Besides, they had noticed he had never missed an evening. He was in love with the game, they said. How could they notice? Didn't they say that "we can't watch each other?" The Balcony Man wondered.

Being very anxious to keep the game going under all circumstances the Balcony Man finally agreed to give them a hand with organizing the Sunnyside.

Before they left they made two suggestions, which were based on the assumption that the Sunnyside and the Shadowside would shortly play one against the other, and they wanted to try out certain techniques. Knowing that most of the other side was playing with the School Teacher's rules, they suggested advising the players on their own side to kiss as much as possible during game time in spite of the Balcony Man's opposition. According to the School Teacher's rules, seeing a couple kissing loses five points. The other suggestion was to cease reading books in the open. School Teacher's rules: reading a book wins twenty-one points.

They went away. The Balcony Man went to the balcony. His wife had gone to bed.

Enid was there. She was sitting on her balcony. Was she crying? He had deserted her. "Enid, I love you. I love you." What was the importance of sides, shadows, suns and all when Enid was crying? "Let the wind carry my whisper to her. I love you, Enid. I love you," whispered the Balcony Man.

Did they see Enid? Did everybody from the Sunnyside see her? They had said so. They had said, "We see the same things."

Now he was alone with Enid. They were watching each other. Enid and he. He was sitting on a chair placed in the same corner of his balcony as Enid's was on hers. Their balconies were identical. She saw hers in his and he saw his in hers. They saw the same things though they belonged to two different sides. She belonged to the Shadowside and he belonged to the Sunnyside.

All of a sudden he heard a bell ringing in one of the apartments on the Shadowside opposite. Hopefully he looked across at Enid's door. It was her bell! He wished he could record it in his memory. He saw her opening the door. Three people entered her flat. So late? They laughed and exchanged words. Enid laughed too. Her laugh! Her laugh! Were they organizing the Shadowside Team? They left. She came back to her balcony.

But the bell! Enid's bell! It sounded different from all the other thousands he had heard in his lifetime. It was the bell of Enid. Automatically he went toward his door. He had to hear his bell. It had to be identical to Enid's. It had to. Otherwise he would search among all the bells of the world until he would find the identical bell to Enid's. He had to do it right now while the sound of her bell was still ringing in his ears. He pressed his bell. It rang. It was identical. Exactly. With uncanny precision. He rang the bell again and again. That was Enid's bell. Her bell rang in his flat. Her bell!

His wife woke up. Who the hell was ringing the bell in the middle of the night? He was! She laughed. Meaningful hint, she said, before coming to bed. They laughed. They put off the light. He got into bed. They came into each other's arms. They slept.

The following evening as the Watching Couple were sitting on their balcony busy with the game, the telephone rang. It was the Balcony Man's turn to get up and take the call. It was somebody whose voice he had never heard before. In a kind of heavy, pleasant voice he said that he was a neighbor from the Shadowside. He said he had got this telephone number by a strange coincidence on which he did not elaborate. "I think it's you I see every evening on your balcony," he said. "You see me too," he continued. "If you come to the balcony and look I'll switch the lights of my flat on and off several times, so you'll know who's speaking, and I'll know whether I've guessed right."

The Balcony Man went to the balcony. His heart trembled. The apartment just below Enid's started to signal with its lights. Yes, he knew the man living there. He had never met him, but he had seen him occasionally while playing the game, and had landed on his windows. He had a wife and two kids. His wife had never played the game. Nor had his kids. Almost every evening he sat by himself for a couple of hours on the balcony and watched other people playing the game. Knowing now who he was the Balcony Man went back to the telephone to hear him say, "I wanted to call somebody opposite me on the Sunnyside and I happened to get you. But I didn't know it was your number. I have guessed wrong. I'm glad it's you."

Through the window the Balcony Man could see him in his room, talking into the telephone, to him! He can also see me, he thought. "I am calling you," said the man, "to ask you to do me a great favor. My wife has heard that the man known as the Second Lonely Gentleman is leaving the housing development. You know he was the assistant of the Lonely Gentleman. The binoculars affair, you know. I have a friend with quite a big family for whom I want to secure this gentleman's apartment. I can't see it as he lives on our side and I wouldn't know whether it's true that he is in fact leaving. From your side you can see him and so you can tell me if there are any signs of his departure. Would you?"

"But I don't know the man," said the Balcony Man, "and I would not know where his apartment is."

"It's very easy," answered the man. "I'll give you a sight-route. If you climb up to the rows of windows above me (Enid! Oh God, Enid!) and go fourteen windows to your right, you'll come to his apartment."

The Balcony Man moved his eyes slowly along, passing the balcony of Enid (she was not there as yet) toward the window of the Second Lonely Gentleman. It would not be altogether true to speak of "his eyes" as, for the moment, they were in some strange way on loan. In a most peculiar fashion and quite unwillingly the Balcony Man became the eyes of the Shadowside Man. Landing on the apartment of the Second Lonely Gentleman, the Balcony Man saw a man preparing to leave the apartment. Nearly everything was packed and he himself was busy trying to close a huge suitcase. Through his binoculars the Balcony Man could even see the happy expression on his face.

Coming back to the telephone he informed the Shadowside Man of his findings.

The Shadowside Man did not have words enough to thank him. He was very excited and offered him his help. "If you ever need anything," he said. Then he gave him his telephone number just in case. They ended the conversation.

Most of the people were already out on their balconies. But it was Enid he was waiting for.

There she was. Smiling. He could see her beautiful smile through his binoculars. Oh, she was beautiful, this girl Enid.

Wasn't divorce the only solution for such a love? But for the Balcony Man it was almost unthinkable. How could he divorce, and face this multitude of people who had been watching him, actually living with him and his wife?

He gradually became aware that the people from the Shadowside, maybe unintentionally, perhaps without malice, were beginning to dictate his life.

Was it what was called a tragic love? Love which could never come to fulfillment, which needed a bridge, but a bridge which no one could ever build?

In his mind the Balcony Man saw that bridge stretching from his balcony to Enid's. He saw Enid and himself walking toward each other to meet in its middle. He heard the public booing. Some, but hardly any, approved. Would not any approval of such an act endanger their own families? Their own lives? Amidst the boos and the shouts Enid and he were coming to each other's arms. Alone on her balcony his wife would become hysterical. The public would identify with her. She was suffering, deserted. People like to see other people suffer. It gives them a strange satisfaction. Happiness was no way with the masses. Happy people are rare, therefore misunderstood and disliked. That was the rule.

The Balcony Man saw the bridge on which Enid and he were standing collapse. They were falling, Enid and he. Hand in hand. That's how their love story would end, if the masses dictated it.

After all, the Balcony Man could take his small valise, go down the stairs, walk the space between the two buildings, be exposed to thousands of eyes, walk up the stairs, enter Enid's room and say, "Here I am." Nothing would happen. No one would kill him. He was free to do so. But the power of the masses did not rest with their guns or bullets. It rested with their eyes, with their persisting binoculars, projecting thousands of years of oppression.

The Balcony Man could not even communicate with Enid, neither by phone nor by letter. He did not even know Enid's name. But if the Shadowside Man could borrow his eyes, he could borrow the Shadowside Man's presence and tongue. He could ask the Shadowside Man to go to Enid, to ask her the questions and tell her the tales. Had not the Shadowside Man offered him his help earlier this evening? No, he could not do that. He would not.

That sonofabitch of a Shadowside Man.

The Balcony Man sat down and started to write a letter.

My dear T.

Many things have happened since you were here last and

got so enthusiastic about the game.

Do you know about my love? I mean the girl you saw while playing with my wife and me last time. You remarked that she must be frigid. A nasty remark, coming from you. But you didn't know then. Nevertheless I love her as I have never loved anyone before. She is a dream which each evening comes true. I stand on the highest point created for men in love. But no. That's not my trouble. I mean, it's part of it. The main thing is rooted in the game.

Recently our side and their side became more or less organized. I was chosen to be the head of the committee on our side, the Sunnyside. Only because we haven't been able to reach agreement over the rules, we haven't played yet against each other but still play individually. But many experiments are being done by both sides in preparation for the time when our side will play against theirs.

I presume it will happen soon. They have adopted the rules of the School Teacher, who lives on their side, the Shadowside. They haven't kept it secret, as we have, but announced it proudly. We are still playing with my original rules. This is not known to their side and it's our big secret. We have chosen this set of rules, just to confuse the "enemy." They will never imagine we are still playing with my rules.

On the other hand we have spread the rumor that we are playing the game according to the rules of the Gentleman Who First Discovered the Watching Couple although he lives on their side and whose rules are the exact opposite of my rules.

Two weeks ago we decided to try to see whether by doing certain things we could make their side lose points. As the School Teacher didn't want to "encourage kissing," he made kissing a loser; a kissing couple meant a loss of five points. Wishing to "encourage reading" he awarded twenty-one points for a person reading.

The committee of our Sunnyside Team decided to recommend certain actions:

1. Throughout the evening the couples from our side should kiss "as much as possible and as often as possible," to inflict losses on the opposite side.

2. People should cease reading books in the open.

There is also a new unwritten rule which says that shades should not be pulled down at any time by someone playing the game. Even if someone does not play the game at certain times the shades in his apartment should be up to allow the players from the other side to play with his apartment.

I am amazed; this rule seems to indicate that once a player always a player.

I personally was against these recommendations but the rest of the committee were strongly for them. We live in a democratic country, unfortunately.

Can you see my dilemma?

I am madly in love with a girl whom I see every evening for hours on end and who sees me. Whom I watch and by whom I am watched, while I am forced to kiss my wife on the grounds that it inflicts losses on the other side. My wife is obeying the instructions so diligently that I wonder whether it is that she loves me so much and is using the game as an opportunity for plenty of kissing, or whether it is the losses to the other side she is thinking of.

The tragedy is complete when I think that my girl on the other side, not knowing of our decision, takes it at face value. I have seen her crying. I can't do anything about it.

Indeed, the situation is too much to bear. I am continually kissing my wife and at the same time loving that beautiful girl across the way.

The only consolation for me lies in the fact that thousands of couples on our side are perpetually kissing each other during game-time and my girl opposite might well have guessed the secret. Who knows?

My daily reading is around fifteen minutes in the toilet, where no one can watch me. Remember! A person reading a book gives twenty-one points to the other side.

Otherwise everything is O.K.

Come over and spend a long weekend with the game. We could have lots of fun.

You can ask me what the hell I am complaining about. I kiss and love, I love and kiss. Oh God!

Yours . . .

And out of the many sighs, sleepless nights, tranquilizers, and millions of words spread abroad by thousands of letters, discussions, day-by-day reports, and personal messages, the housing development emerged, tired but happy, organized into two teams.

Many problems cropped up and were solved. Although some of the problems arising from the new situation were quite serious for those directly involved, the estate took everything in good part and with lots of laughter. A new brand of joke appeared and swept the area. A new kind of game-lore gradually grew up.

A spectacular march by all the school children symbolized the new era. It was a sensational parade through the housing development, ending in the school yard. All the youngsters carried banners saying, "We are with you, skipper," 'skipper' being the Headmaster. It needed no explanation. The Headmaster, living on the Sunnyside where a lot of kissing was going on, was at once identified with those who had favored kissing when the kissing issue arose.

Shouts of laughter engulfed the housing development when the School Teacher from the Shadowside made a heart-rending speech from the top of the school steps to the youngsters telling them that he was ready to take on the Headmaster in a kissing-match.

"Our respected Headmaster is an excellent scholar but a very poor kisser," he ended his speech.

The Headmaster was unaware of the Sunnyside committee's Kissing Directive, as he was one of the few who had no real interest in the game. Suddenly he found himself fêted by all the younger generation and by many of the aging inhabitants. Not understanding this sudden wave of admiration, the Headmaster declared happily that this was a clear sign that intellect was triumphing over ignorance. But when informed of the real issue and of the School Teacher's speech, he was furious. "He should get in some practice before he starts boasting that he has won the match," he exclaimed. "The young are our future and our hope. They have shown where they stand. After all, they are the ones to decide who is the winner."

The School Teacher, realizing that he had achieved exactly the opposite of what he had aimed at when changing the original rules, as lots of kissing was going on among the players (and not only on the Sunnyside), called a public meeting to discuss the "Moral Aspects of the Game." He was afraid to change back to the original rules and so encourage lots of kissing on his own side. As a result he became utterly confused. The fact that there was no record of any people being seen reading also counted against him and made his confusion greater.

In the meantime, the two sides were drifting more and more apart. In the most natural way the people of each side started to visit their own particular shops and gas stations. Names like the "Sunnyside Supermarket" or the "Shadowside Gas Station" were spreading fast. The Gentleman from the Bar, not willing to lose customers of either side, jokingly divided the week into three: the Sunnyside Days, the Shadowside, Days, and the Kissing Days. Being himself from the Shadowside, he employed a man from the Sunnyside to join him in running the bar.

During that period, somebody even put up a small sign at the entrance to the housing development, which read: "Visit the Shadowside," opposite which was scrawled: "For top-quality kissing, visit the Sunnyside."

No one actually knew why, by whom, or with what intention those signs had been erected. While the argument about it was going on, someone putting up a new sign which read "Knock on any door and get a warm welcome from the Sunnyside people," was caught red-handed. The housing development swiftly learned that the man was none other than the Gentleman from the Post. The most amazing thing of all was that he himself lived on the Shadowside, whereas his sign was complimentary to the opposite side. No one doubted his integrity or his honesty, but it seemed to many people, especially those on his own side, a betrayal of the confidence they had placed in him since the difficult days of the Watching Couple.

On the other hand groups of people from the Sunnyside kept coming to congratulate him on his tolerance and he received many letters of appreciation. His own side was getting angrier and angrier with him and he could not stand it any longer. In an unusual effort to justify himself in the eyes of his side he declared that by placing the signs asking visitors to visit the other side he was thinking only of the benefit they would bring to his own side. "By people visiting their side and entering their apartments, we could win points, as according to our rules every person seen in the flats opposite wins us more points."

When his confession became known, the feelings of both sides toward him changed completely. The people of his own side went out of their way to show him their trust and renewed confidence. Many flowers, letters, and presents arrived at his flat. The Sunnyside people were ashamed to admit their failure, and the short love affair between them and the Gentleman from the Post vanished as if it had never been.

The Game Papers

It was a Friday when a copy of the secret research on the game, commissioned by the police a few months before, was leaked to the local daily and was instantly published in full. Because other national papers took up the issue, for the first time the game started to be noticed by the outside world.

There was a stormy discussion in the housing development concerning the Game Papers. People were angered and irritated. The research carried on by TREED (Total Research on Essentially Everything Department) began with a general outlook on the game. "We think of The Game in terms of BLOCK CULTURE."

This sentence alone was explosive. "Are we treated as a mass?" "Do we belong to a block culture?" were only some of the comments.

The research went on to say:

> Even if everybody in the housing development started to play The Game, it would not limit its possibilities as life has to go on inside the various apartments.
>
> A few years ago we published our findings on *Life and*

Its Advantages which was sponsored by the Ministry of War for its information center. This included a special chapter on "Expected and Unexpected Factors in Life." There we came to the conclusion that life consists of 91 per cent unexpected happenings, leaving only 9 per cent expected.

According to these figures, even allowing for slight modifications in recent years, we think that the unexpected element will make The Game playable even if everybody plays it.

In other words, the suburbanites, even if playing The Game, would have to cope with unexpected things. They would have to receive guests, 39.55 per cent of whom come unexpectedly (see *Expected and Unexpected Factors in Life*, page 91), and would have to entertain them. They would have to give birth to children (37 per cent unexpected), to bring them up, attend to their wishes (54 per cent unexpected), treat their maladies, call doctors, and so on.

The Game, apart from being pure and harmless entertainment, carries many obvious advantages, social, psychological, economic, sexual, and political.

Almost every point of the Game Papers turned out to be a public irritant.

The Papers were divided into five parts each of which spoke of different advantages of the game.

The first part dealt with the social advantages. It was like gunpowder.

Social Advantages

The Game creates evening gatherings of people whose aim is to indulge in an innocent amusement after a hard day's work.

It will make people look at, and eventually see, each other.

It will make people take each other at face value.

It will make people see some of the problems their neighbors have and thus get involved in them. This will inevitably inspire in each individual a feeling of responsibility for his neighbors and ultimately for the whole community.

It will create a feeling of a united community.

It will reduce crime to a minimum, as everyone will be watched by everyone else all the time.

The closely watched family unit will become healthier by not having the chance to experience all kinds of vice and violence so common nowadays. Thus:

A. Men will hardly allow themselves to be seen beating their wives or vice versa.

B. Wives will hardly allow lovers and other notorious types to enter their bedrooms.

C. Children on the threshold of puberty will stop masturbating and using unnatural devices.

D. Each family will have to keep its apartment spick and span. They will be forced to clean it every day, and thus babies will have a healthier and cleaner upbringing.

E. Help, if needed, will be rendered within minutes by the people around, as they are constantly on the scene.

F. People from different classes, different walks of life, and wearing different collars, white, blue, black, or pink, will get to know, understand, and probably forgive each other.

G. Instead of the difficult problem of communicating with each other by leaving their apartments "to go neighboring," people will now sit on their balconies and exchange glances in comfort.

H. People will think twice before doing something which might give the block a bad reputation.

Conclusion: The Game will force people into honest social behavior. All for one and one for all.

There was no end to the discussions. It was the Light Gentleman who took over the leadership concerning the Game Papers.

He became known as the Light Gentleman of the Game Papers.

A few hours after the research had been published the Light Gentleman stood in the middle of the main street of the housing development and delivered an angry speech. From their balconies people started to shout in protest against the Game Papers. It was getting dark and more and more people were coming out onto their balconies. At one point the scene resembled an ancient Roman arena with crowds of people sitting in the tribunes all around while one man was fighting in the middle. Maybe this sight was what inspired the Reverend to approach the Light Gentleman and propose to him to go up to the church tower and continue to deliver his message to the people with the help of a microphone.

The church was situated just at the end of the main street and its tower overlooked most of the balconies of the housing development.

Now almost everybody could hear the LG say, "Only a silly game can inspire such an insulting and inhuman document as the Game Papers."

Because none of the people could make himself heard they started to write various comments on large sheets of paper, holding them above their heads. Some of the placards read:

"Is our Reverend for or against the game?"

"If our Lord Jesus Christ were alive what would He have thought of the game?"

Most people felt that the trouble with the research was that it treated people as objects who did not display a will of their own or any individual character. That was made clear in the part dealing with the psychological advantages.

Psychological Advantages

The Game will create an outlet for the people's suppressed

curiosity.

It will free them from their most common fear—not knowing what is going on in the other apartments.

It will give them a feeling of security and the dangerous feeling of isolation will disappear.

Each one will visually experience a feeling of belonging.

As a member of a whole community (now visible), the individual will develop greater self-confidence and feelings of inferiority will eventually fade away.

By learning to control their aggressions and unnatural desires, as a direct result of The Game, people will become desirable elements in the structure of society.

Man's inner self will eventually grow cleaner, healthier, and more mature.

The dangerous "apartment psychosis" and the various apartment complexes will disappear completely as people realize that everybody else lives in an apartment identical to his own.

This will create a healthy community.

Through the microphone the Reverend told the people that he was not against the game in any way but felt that a man such as the Light Gentleman, so obsessed against the game and the Game Papers, must be given the opportunity to be heard. He called upon the people for tolerance, and requested "anybody who has anything to say" to come up to the tower.

Some people took the opportunity and went up the church tower to deliver their message to the housing development. All of them were in favor of the game but strongly against the Game Papers.

From their speeches it became clear that what most annoyed the population were the parts concerning the economic, sexual, and political advantages:

Economic Advantages

The Game is an evening entertainment which, apart from its amusement value, will serve to unite families and create stronger ties between their members.

Husbands will no longer feel the need to frequent places of notoriety in the evenings and to stay out all night. This will increase the birth rate, which, needless to say, is most beneficial to society, economically speaking.

This Game, by its very nature, can and will teach people to be alert and open to critical sightseeing. This alertness, if used rightly by the government, can produce beneficial results: for example, good soldiers, good workers, and disciplined citizens.

If The Game catches on, it will encourage people to buy apartments in the housing developments. In order to buy these apartments people will need large loans from the banks. To repay these loans, people will have to work harder and be more productive, to the advantage of the economy of our state and of our society.

The Game will force people to enter the class race. They will have to start worrying about their social status—they will of course have to furnish and decorate their apartments accordingly. They will have to buy pictures for the walls, large refrigerators for the kitchens, carpets for the floors, china for the mantelpieces, good furniture, impressive chandeliers, fashionable games for their children, and silver cutlery. This is all to the economic advantage of our state and of our society.

Conclusion: The Game will increase our birth rate, our manpower, and the amount of money in circulation.

Sexual Advantages

The Game will fill a gap in the life of contemporary society. It will provide people with new values and take their interest off sex-motivated activities such as the "Gay Society," "Women's Lib Movement," the "Transvestites group," etc.

Inevitably this will create the KEEP-IT-COOL SOCIETY.

The keep-it-cool society means a healthy path to normalization of sex relations. Sex will become what it originally was meant for: a harmless act of producing the next generation.

Conclusion: Sex will cease to be a leading factor in the life of our contemporary society. Thus people will be free to concentrate upon more important matters.

Political Advantages

Every politician prefers, of course, what is termed VOTING BLOCKS, mainly because these can be reached more easily during election campaigns.

The Game serves this purpose well.

In due time the government can levy a new tax called "The Playing Flat Tax." Thus, the government will considerably increase its revenue.

General Advice:

We recommend that The Game be allowed to grow and take its own course without any interference from the police or any other officiant body.

We condemn the use of The Game for any purposes incompatible with the progress of a modern society such as ours.

The police should not use information obtained as a result of The Game.

Income Tax officials should also be warned not to use The Game for their own purposes.

It should not be forgotten that The Game was invented purely as an entertainment and should remain such.

We advise the police to ask a few responsible building residents to keep day-by-day reports over the coming months.

We also recommend that further research be carried out

in the course of the next six months. The day-by-day reports might be of help.

At the end of this report you will find several diagrams and tables:

A. On Rates of Loneliness.

B. On Rates of Boredom.

C. On Time.

Concerning the Lonely Gentleman (the binoculars salesman) we could find no clause by which one could press charges against him. We found out that he had served only six weeks in the army and was ultimately discharged for endlessly inciting violence and the killing of the enemy.

In his army file we found the following statement: "He was creating a bad name for the army and was therefore discharged."

As obviously one cannot make a bad name for the army in willing to kill the enemy we found that the Lonely Gentleman had intended to sell binoculars to the soldiers and officers using the slogan, "See better—Kill better." That was taken literally by the army, which did not know of his commercial intention.

The report has the approval of the Commissioner and of the Superintendent and is dated 10th September.

Top Secret. Sensitive.

The Rev-Ref

The Sunnyside team and the Shadowside team were ready to play their first match. But not exactly. There were still some problems which had to be surmounted. Too many people were annoyed for different reasons, too many people felt that the real decisions concerning the game had been taken without their participation, too many opposed the game altogether, and too many wished to express in words their feelings toward the game and had never had the opportunity. An encounter between the dissatisfied and the two committees was arranged. The local bar seemed to be the best choice for such a confrontation.

Another problem was the Referee. The game between the two teams could not have its debut without a Referee. The committees of both sides decided to carry on a sort of election for a Referee. There were no candidates but each player could vote for any person he saw fit.

On the day of the meeting the bar was crowded. The School Teacher was there, outraged because both committees recommended that the game be played with the Balcony Man's rules. Opposing every bit of the game, the Light Gentleman was there.

Shocked by the accusations made against him, the Peeping Tom was there. Bewildered by the whole issue, especially by the challenge of the School Teacher for the kissing match, the Headmaster was there. The two Supermarket Ladies, who had just recently opened a bureau for an organized struggle against the game's rule concerning Black people, also were there.

Out of loyalty for his folk the Reverend was there. He intended to be a bridge between the parties. There were also quite a few unidentified residents of the housing development. And of course the members of the two committees: The GD, the GP, and the GB from the Shadowside, and the Balcony Man with three aides from the Sunnyside.

Before the meeting got under way, people had been engaged over an article published in the local newspaper saying that the Lonely Gentleman, who had left the housing development after the binoculars affair had become known, was writing a book about the first stages of the game, including the famous binoculars sale. It also said that one of the respectable publishers in the city was interested in the property. Everyone in the bar put forward an opinion on the affair. In that sense the Lonely Gentleman was also present there.

The Gentleman from the Bar opened the official meeting. "Well," he said, "at last we're organized into two teams. We still have some problems, but we're all confident we'll solve them, too. In about an hour we're going to have the results of the Referee's election. People are invited to speak out their minds concerning the game. Please, try to cut your speeches short and do not raise new problems . . ."

"Now let me tell you, sons of nincompoops," shouted the Light Gentleman, who was drunk, "you are going to destroy the whole of civilization and you are so damn blind that you don't even see it!"

"How on earth can a game destroy civilization? Football

didn't!" said the GB.

"Let me tell you," the LG was carried away, "you bunch of eggnog heads, you bunch of pretzel eaters, you rot of delicatessen sniffers, you are right! The game cannot destroy civilization. It was destroyed long ago. To be exact, the day you were born."

"Oh, God!"

"Explain!"

"He's drunk, can't you see?"

"Keep it cool, will you!"

"Well," the LG went on, "can you imagine just a few months ago if somebody had stared at everything inside your apartment with a pair of binoculars. What would you have done? Call the police? But then imagine the police telling you that they've nothing against people peeping inside the various apartments. Then you'd probably call your lawyer just to hear him laugh and say, 'Let him watch. What d'you care?' Then you'd call your therapist to tell him you have been hearing voices telling you inconceivable things. Isn't that right . . . ?"

"That's wrong!"

"You are a bunch of Peeping Toms!" shouted the Light Gentleman.

"What?" cried the Peeping Tom. "I protest! I protest!"

"Please," desperately pleaded the GB, "please keep cool. Please."

"I protest!" continued the Peeping Tom. "My integrity has been challenged!"

"What does he mean?" asked the Supermarket Lady.

"I don't understand," said the Second Supermarket Lady.

"I want an apology," cried the Peeping Tom. "I have been put in prison for what is practiced today by the respected classes. I don't want to be offended and called a Peeping Tom in a negative way!"

"Please calm down!" said the GB. "He didn't mean you alone,

he called all of us Peeping Toms."

"Sure," cried the Peeping Tom, "you can take it. I am the only one who cannot take it, because unlike you I am a real Peeping Tom."

"What?"

"That's not true!"

"What do you mean you're a real Peeping Tom?" asked the Headmaster.

"I had been one even before the game started," said the Peeping Tom. "Then I did just what I do today, with one difference. Today I am proud of it. I was here before you, and was martyred for it! And my father before me!"

"Oh God almighty!"

"That's the proof gentlemen," said the Light Gentleman. "Stop the game, go back to your television sets, it's incomparably healthier. Halt this mutual watching, which is going to produce incurable imbeciles . . ."

"Please gentlemen," said the School Teacher, "it seems that the issues are all mixed up. The gentleman who has presented himself as a Peeping Tom has done so, I believe, only for metaphorical purposes, to express the absurdities of a society which changes its code of morals. Now my rules . . ."

"What do you mean by metaphorical purposes?" asked the Headmaster.

"To teach us a lesson."

"But the man has said he was a Peeping Tom, hasn't he?"

"I was a Peeping Tom. I am not any longer," said the Peeping Tom sadly.

"Oh good," said the School Teacher. "I am glad you got rid of your habit."

"Not at all, gentlemen," said the Peeping Tom. "You've accepted it as a part of our culture."

"Well, nonetheless, let's go back to our real issue," said the

School Teacher, who was impatient to change the subject. "My rules are based on the moral values of the individual. They will afford each person freedom for individual expression. But instead, you intend to take a set of rules which make one big identical mass of our society. Even Communism would be too mild a word for it . . ."

"In any game you have one set of rules!" said the GD.

"You couldn't play football for instance, with each player having his own rules," said the GP.

"But we could make a game in which it would be possible!" said the School Teacher.

"How?"

"Yes how?"

Suddenly the Balcony Man stood up and raised his hand requesting permission to speak. There was silence. The Balcony Man was calm: "Gentlemen, the rules of the environment are the rules of the game. What I mean is this. The game has been invented, that's a fact; people have liked it and have probably even felt it gives them a way to express themselves. Man has created an environment in which a wonderful game has been hidden. Man has discovered it and is using it most likely for his own survival. The game has become a part of the same environment which has been hiding it . . ."

"Is that progress?" shouted the Light Gentleman.

"You might not like it but you have to consider it. You can't say let's forget it and go back to the TV sets."

"I still say let's go back."

"We can't go back. We are not the same people now that we know the game . . ."

"Bravo."

"Hear! Hear!"

"The housing development," said the Balcony Man, "did not conceal in it an individual game. It was a mass game. As I said, the rules of the environment are the rules of the game, identical and good for everybody. There was nothing individual in that environment. I discovered, by mere chance, the only game which reflected our culture."

Outside the bar the "election " for the Referee was conducted in the most simple manner. A few youngsters ran from door to door asking the tenants for their vote. When most of the apartments were visited, it became clear that the election was a total failure. There were no candidates, and everyone made his individual choice. Most of them gave the name of their neighbor or of themselves. In that way the greatest number of votes for one person was nineteen. This number could not be taken as representing the majority's choice.

When the youngsters arrived at the bar with the election results, one of the Supermarket Ladies was making her maiden speech. From it there was no doubt that everything that was wrong in the world, everything that caused pain, suffering and torment, the existence of the Spanish Inquisition, and the invention of the guillotine, were due to the game's Negro rule.

Hardly anybody was paying any attention to her. People were drinking and joking with each other.

"Well, what about the Ref?" asked the GD after a while.

"What about him?" asked the GP.

"We haven't got him yet," said the GD.

"Oh, you mean the Ref," said the GP.

"Sure, who else?"

"I thought you said the Rev. I was just looking at him," said the GP.

"No, I said the Ref, not the Rev."

"I have it! I have it!" enthusiastically cried the GB. "The Rev is the Ref."

"What?"

"Why not?"

"You mean the Rev should Ref?"

"That's not a bad idea," said the GD.

"He might not like it," remarked the GP.

"We'd better ask him," said the GB, and went to the Reverend's table. "Well, Father," opened the GB, "none of our problems seemed to be solved. We thought of something and wanted to ask your opinion. We wanted you to be the Referee of the game."

"Me?"

"Sure, why not?"

"Well, I suppose you're right. Why not?"

"Are you willing to?"

"I don't know . . . I must think, decide . . . I don't know . . ."

"Please, Rev. Everybody would be quite happy if you took the job."

"To be a Referee to a game? It's so far from my faith . . . from my being a priest . . ."

Overhearing the conversation, the Balcony Man moved a few steps toward the Reverend's table.

"There are two pros to consider, Father," said the Balcony Man. "One is that you would make people happy by becoming their Referee. Making people happy can't be against your faith or against your priesthood."

"That's true," said the Reverend thoughtfully.

"Second," continued the Balcony Man, "excuse the thought, but isn't a priest a sort of a Referee between Heaven and Earth?"

People standing around started laughing. The bar seemed to have become a laughing bar. It also seemed that the problems, or at least the major ones, were on their way to being solved. Everyone knew that if the Reverend would become the Referee he would decide on everything and his solutions would be accepted willingly by all.

The Reverend looked around him. People started to applaud. He felt he was loved, respected, and trusted. There was no real reason not to accept the offer. Besides, he thought, it would give him an extra point of contact with his people and would open additional possibilities for communication. He stood up.

"I accept," he said. "So help me God."

For a few days the new Referee, or the Rev-Ref, as he was called, held meetings with players of both sides who had problems which were directly connected with the game. The Rev-Ref's decisions were final. He permitted the Light Gentleman to go on protesting against the game, in whichever form he chose. The original rules of the Balcony Man were adopted for a trial period of six months. To that even the School Teacher agreed.

It was decided that the game would be played seven days a week, between 7:30 P.M. and midnight. The mode of playing the game in its new form—the Sunnyside against the Shadowside—was established.

Dice were thrown by each playing unit—one balcony or one apartment—in a prearranged order. The number on the dice was to be communicated by the player who had thrown the dice to the players on the opposite side by flickering the light of the balcony or by a flashlight. All the players on the first side would start "to go windows" according to the number of the dice. As each player would have a different starting point, quite a great number of windows would be covered.

The Rev-Ref, who turned the tower of his church into his Referee quarters, could stop the game at any moment and with the use of his loudspeaker ask a certain player how many points he had won. The answer would be communicated to the Rev-Ref by the same system of flickering the lights.

The winning scores of each unit on one side were to be combined for the total result of each team. The daily results were announced the next day, a half hour before the start of the game. The weekly results were announced at noon on Sundays, accompanied by a game sermon, hymn, and prayer.

The winning team would receive a flag, to be flown from one of its balconies.

Each month an individual cup for the player who scored most of the points for his team would be awarded by the Rev-Ref.

Outside the official time of the game, everyone was free to go on playing the game individually. People who did not want to participate in the game or to be watched by others could draw their curtains. However, three hours during the day, between noon and three o'clock, no one was allowed to play the game, in order to enable these people to draw open their curtains and enjoy their daily portion of daylight.

The first few matches were set aside for trying out the game, but in a short while most of the people in the housing development plunged into the game with growing excitement.

For three weeks daily matches were played between the Sunnyside and the Shadowside. For three weeks in succession the Sunnyside lost the game and the flag fluttered high from one of the balconies of the Shadowside.

The Shadowside Against the Sunnyside

For the first time since the daily matches began the Balcony Man realized that he no longer watched only the windows he landed on during the game; suddenly he had become aware of the whole of the other side.

For the first time he saw not only one cell encased within itself but thousands of them, forming an inseparable unity. A unity with its own atmosphere, rhythm, and way of life.

Instantly he realized that the people of the other side felt the same way toward his side. He began to wonder how his side appeared in their eyes. What actually happened on his side? Was his side a sad or happy side? Dramatic or pathetic? Who loses points? Who gives points? While he knew everything about their side, he did not know a single thing about his own side. Did he fit into the pattern of his side, or was he a foreigner to the whole picture?

For the last three weeks his side had been losing. Who was to blame? Was it he? How did one learn about one's own side?

Voices of the Sunnyside

Last night we discovered that there is a Jewish family on our side. They gather every Friday night to see the Sabbath in. Fifteen or twenty people reading prayers before dinner from books is a real disaster. One person reading a book gives three points to the other side.

Oi! Gewalt!

Voices of the Shadowside

Today we have discovered the ex-big-game hunter who lives on our side. He has one small tiger, a rare bird, two snakes, a monkey, one chicken, sole survivor of a lost species, and a turkey. He apologized for the turkey which, he explained, he was keeping for Christmas. We talked to him quite frankly. We told him that every player landing on his window gave the other side at least a hundred points. It was a disaster. He knew it, he said.

As if that was not enough, we made the acquaintance of an unmarried girl who has a black boyfriend. Not only that, but sometimes he brings some of his friends with him. He lives on the Sunnyside but every evening he comes to our side to visit his fiancée. Can't she go and visit him? She says no, as his family is not so favorably inclined to their association. We are meeting tonight after the official finish of the game to discuss the situation.

Somebody told us of a certain boy who is going to have a birthday. Nothing alarming about that, except that his parents are planning a birthday party. Birthday party!

Voices of the Sunnyside

A prostitute on our side! Shame! Shame! We talked to her. Personally she was very nice and accommodating, and we cannot cut her off from her source of income, can we? She meets her customers down in the main road and brings them here. Ten to fifteen every evening. Very successful! She turns the lights on and off approximately forty times per evening. Quite often a man is seen in his underwear, passing the window (six points!).

What can she do? She can't deprive the men of their freedom. One should be able to walk about in whatever one likes. That is her trademark: freedom. She understands. It might come to ninety points an evening. She knows.

A prostitute on our side! Even this we could forgive, but all those losses.

We are forming a committee to solve this problem.

From the prostitute we have heard about a wedding. Wedding!? On our side? With guests and all? With presents? Books? Silver? China? Who the hell gets married these days? This is the age of lovers! Fools! At least two-hundred points! At least! They may even get a huge refrigerator as a present. Hell! We ought to have chosen a better side to live on. This is the side of losers.

Learning that a Negro lives on our side made our hearts beat faster. Fifteen points! We are going crazy. We have nothing against Negroes. Some of our best friends are Negroes. But on our side? It's an old problem, the Negro problem. We know. Our housing development is tolerant. Nobody here minds Negroes, Jews, communists, or homosexuals. Really! Go and explain that to a Negro.

We talked to him. He said somebody from the other side had already talked to him. From the other side? What the hell are they talking to people from our side for? He has a girl friend on the other side. Yes. Every evening he goes there. Good! Good! Wonderful! He goes to the other side! Every evening! That's it! That's the right thing to do, man! One should go there. What have they told you? The people from the other side? What? What? The hypocrites! They want you to stay in your own place! The white pigs! The racists! Everyone has the right to move around as much as he likes! Hell! The world is your place, man! You should move. God gave roots to trees, to men he gave legs. You better believe it! Take some of your friends along. Show them you are not an idiot! You are a man who does what he likes! And he likes to go to the other side. Show them. The creeps!

Voices of the Shadowside

We are going crazy. Every hour we hear of a new disaster. Now it is that woman who insists on having her baby at home. She is in her ninth month. Any minute now. Doctor with instruments: five points; with white robe: twenty-three points. Nurse with white robe: fifty-one points. Two nurses: one hundred two points. God!

But lady . . . nowadays? Everybody goes to the hospital nowadays. Nice hospitals. Warm! With lots of flowers! They are everywhere! The Stone Age has passed. Long ago. Babies are not born at home any more. They can't be. We know! They refuse to come out. We assure you! Tradition? Yes, very important. But look here lady, tradition must be logical. It must go with the times! Okay, you were born at home, your mother, too. Really? Your grandmother and your great-grandmother? But those times were different. Of course we are not against tradition. We are not out of our minds. Tradition is not bad but there must be some sense of proportion. We know about the comforts. We assure you. But hospitals are nice nowadays too. With other women in your room so you are never alone. Gossip? No! No, madam! We didn't mean gossip. We meant fun. We meant the fun of not being alone. But madam, the baby can't see for the first month. It says so in all the books. We assure you, it won't know the difference. No, we can't remember, but we know . . .

And after the Home Confinement Lady, we are confronted with a family that is planning a masked ball for their three insistent children. Aged sixteen, seventeen, and eighteen.

The father understands. He has no say in the matter. How

many young people are coming? He does not know. Will they kiss each other? Nowadays one never can tell. Anything is possible. One cannot stop time. The father is a kind of modern philosopher. His children should be free. He suffers, of course, but that is life.

Today it is better to be a son or a daughter than a father. Sure, he is still responsible for them. But kissing is their own business. When he was young himself he hadn't minded the kissing. On the contrary. But now? How many points? Ten couples kissing, while the rest are dancing—one of them might be eating . . . Oh! All those points! We might lose this week simply because of this. Yes! It is possible. That's fate. One can't control fate.

We are trying to find a solution to all these problems.

Voices of the Sunnyside

Our side is thrilled to learn the true facts about itself. We decided to have a regular tax. The Game Tax. Everybody agreed. The tax was needed to solve the soluble problems. They were only a few. The rest could not be solved. Not with money, anyway. We couldn't evacuate the Jewish family, or redeem the prostitute, or separate the marrying couple. We had to live with them all. But we could solve some of the problems. Every Friday there was a couple playing cards with another couple from the city. We offered them four tickets for the opera every Friday. They agreed. The Game Tax helped here. We booked a weekly subscription for them for the opera. Now they are opera lovers. What else?

Next, we rented a bus for a whole evening to take out a party of old army friends of some sergeant who was planning to have them at home. He was said to be very old. No wonder. The First World War, and he still had a busful of friends. Funny, isn't it? First World War. He needs these reunions. Once a year, his wife explained. It's the anniversary of the day on which he managed something heroic on the battlefield. All those years, and he still could not remember exactly what it was. His comrades refused to tell him. They liked to tease him. Now the bus is taking them around. Otherwise, one hundred twenty points at least. Some of the people might also turn up in their old uniforms. And that, point-wise, would be disastrous.

Every evening, before the official start of the game, we would go and meet some of the Problem People of our side. We wouldn't miss a game.

Today we approached the Jewish family. We had some gefilte-fish. They explained their faith. Money could not buy that. We only asked them if they could learn the prayers by heart, so they would not be seen with all these books around. They laughed a lot. They were kind. They did not want money. They would try, they said. It is not so difficult to learn prayers by heart. Especially not if you believe in them.

Voices of the Shadowside

Saturday. The week's results up till now are in our favor. Tomorrow the weekly winner will be decided. We will know on which side the flag is to flutter for another week.

But alas. We have five birthdays on our side. Today! Why are people born on Saturdays? It should be forbidden. We have tried to cancel them, without success. One cannot actually cancel somebody's birthday. They have promised to be careful not to make us lose too many points. We'll see.

Voices of the Sunnyside

Saturday. We must win tonight. We have drawn up a plan. Top secret.

Voices of the Shadowside

Saturday. Two birthdays less. We hired a hall in town for them. We have a special collection for such cases. We must win.

Voices of the Sunnyside

Saturday. It is working! It is working, for Christ's sake! It is working! Our plan is working.

Voices of the Shadowside

Saturday evening. What? What is the meaning of this? No, I don't need any monkeys. No, I didn't order them in town. Not at all. Please, will you take them out of my flat! No, I have never asked anyone to bring me monkeys and unleash them in my flat. No, I don't care to see if they like it. I don't give a damn if they like it or not! I am not interested. Take them out of here at once. They are on the balcony! Good Heavens! What the hell is this?

When did I decide to carry out such an experiment? Never! I detest animals. Especially monkeys. Particularly this kind of monkey. If I want to buy monkeys I'll get in touch with the zoo. No, I have never asked the zoo to send anybody to me. In any case not at this hour of the night. Hell! Am I going out of my mind? I am telling you, I have never written to you. Never. I don't even know who the hell you are. If this is a joke, I don't see it. You hear? You will not succeed in getting rid of your monkeys here. Three monkeys! You don't say. Take them out of here. I am not interested in their origin. Nor in mine. I'll call the police! Out!

Voices of the Sunnyside

Saturday evening. It's wonderful! Wonderful! What a sight! The best sight in town. All our side is roaring with laughter. You can hear the whole community is laughing. It was a brilliant idea. What a view. What a spectacle!

It must make us win. It must. All these monkeys jumping around the flats on the other side make one's heart bound.

In at least twenty flats, at least one monkey is jumping around. One monkey: eighteen points. We must win this game. It's certain we will. One of our side landed on a flat where four monkeys, the monkey salesman, and the head of the family were present. While he was still there, the young son of the family was woken up and came in half naked while the wife, carrying a coffee tray to the balcony, dropped it when she found herself face to face with the monkeys. Out of this alone we made more than a hundred points.

How did we come upon that idea? To send letters to all the monkey dealers in town! About sixty letters. More than twenty came. It was the letter that did it. The letter read:

Dear Sir,

I am writing to you on behalf of my neighbors, who would like to have some sample monkeys delivered to their house on approval. The family in question is a bit strange, especially the man, but he is in no way dangerous. He is mad about monkeys and would like to have a few around. But for some reason or other he is ashamed of it. He is particularly ashamed of making this desire known. Therefore we took it upon ourselves to write this letter.

This is a well-known phenomenon in our experience of psychiatry—especially in man-monkey relationships.

The man is practically in love with monkeys. But when confronted with them he gets a bit nervous. He might even shout or seem to lose his temper. But this is not serious and passes as soon as the man feels that the monkeys are at home in his presence.

Under the circumstances we kindly request you to visit the family at the above-mentioned address and take with you at least two monkeys.

Five is the limit.

You must understand that we cannot promise you a sale. This must be left solely to the parties concerned. We advise you to be on your guard when the said gentleman opens the door. At this moment you should unleash the monkeys, in spite of his protests, which we hope we have made clear are not serious at all, and let them free in his flat. He will shout, might even curse, but do not worry, this is his way. Explain carefully something of the nature of monkeys and their origin. That will be enough. Forgive him in advance for any coarse words he might use. He will certainly apologize later. Tomorrow evening between eight-thirty and ten-thirty will be the most suitable time for such a visit.

Yours sincerely,

P.S. If this family declines the monkeys for some reason, we advise you to try other doors in that block as there are many animal lovers among them.

Sunday. We have won! We have won! The flag is fluttering high above our side. For the first time since the start of the game. We have won! What a triumph! We have won with a laugh. It's much better winning with a laugh. What a laugh! The Shadowside is so angry. So pathetically miserable. Today we started the score for another week. For a whole week the flag is on our side. What a triumph! That monkey business! That's what did it.

Voices of the Shadowside

The cheats! The brutes! The fools! Monkey business! Ugh! It's not funny at all. So they won, so what! We have won up till now. Once in a while we can afford to lose.

Now the game is taking another turn. It's no longer merely a matter of luck. It's not even skill. It's cunning! O.K. Monkey business! They won. But if that's the way they want to play, we won't lag far behind.

Monday. The police station.

The head of the Negro department please. Negro department? We have no such department. But you have black policemen who deal with the Negro sections of the city, don't you? Oh, yes. Could we speak to their head? Do you have an appointment? No. Just a moment.

A black policeman comes over.

What can I do for you? There are many families among us who should get better acquainted with the Negro problem. Most people have no idea about these problems. So we decided to suggest that you organize a kind of lecture tour to explain to our people your point of view. We cannot expect a better explanation of the situation. You understand! You are in the know! You know the pains, the hopes, the unfulfilled dreams those people have. Their difficulties, their daily misfortunes in our wretched white society. Which white society? Ours. Our heartless white society. What can we do for you? If you could send some policemen from your department to explain to us the situation . . .

The address is the Sunnyside! Any flat! They cannot refuse you, can they? They must listen to you. Even if some of them are not interested. They will have to listen. You can call it "An Explanatory Lecture Tour." It would also give the police a good name. We know! Of course you already have a good name. But it might turn the good to a better.

You understand that we cannot be responsible for the outcome. We hope you appreciate this. We think that the people need a good lecture tour. They are ignorant. You can tell them.

When?

Tonight.

Voices of the Sunnyside

What is the matter, sir? No, we don't need any lectures. We know. We understand the situation! It's difficult and painful, we know. Unbearable, one might say. We know. People just don't understand. It's wicked and inhuman. If we hadn't known, we would have liked to hear what you have to say. We are not blocking the door. Not at all. You can come in if you must. You are the police after all!

Voices of the Shadowside

Ha! Ha! At least twenty black policemen in groups of three are entering the flats of the Sunnyside. They have come to give their lecture! Ha! Lecture away, boys, and we'll rake in the points.

That ought to be enough for this week.

Voices of the Sunnyside

Never mind! Let's see who wins in the end. So they've landed us with Negro policemen. But are there enough people at home on the Shadowside tonight to win the points?

Voices of the Shadowside

What? The theater? What kind of theater? No! What? People getting free tickets for the theater? Why didn't we know about it? But anyhow who is interested in the theater nowadays? What? How many? Hundred and twenty of them? They couldn't resist the temptation of such an honor and stay at home! What the hell! The theater is dead! We know! We have read it in the newspapers! They know! That is their misfortune! I am telling you—the theater is dead, and any that are still functioning should be killed off. Sure. What? *The Wild Duck?* Drama! Absolute rubbish!

Voices of the Sunnyside

It has worked again! Eureka! The theater is empty, it is dying. We offered them a large and enthusiastic audience. We paid a bit, of course. But not much. Theater People are beggars. It is well known. The money came from the Game Tax. We composed the invitation and put inside it the tickets we had bought.

It is a trial performance given to test the play's appeal, and therefore only a carefully selected audience is being invited.

We count on your presence! etc. etc.

They all went, poor souls. *The Wild Duck!* Oh! Hedvig! Ha!

Voices of the Shadowside

Hundred and twenty families less! It's terrible! Who could have known they like the theater, the fools. We are going to lose again. The Negro policemen with their clever talk! Hell! It does not help much. How can it help if there are not enough people to win the points? We are going to lose!

Voices of the Sunnyside

We've won! We've won again! The flag stays on our side. We can always win now. All you need is the right ideas!

Tonight is the monthly presentation of the individual cups to the winners on each side. The ceremony is to take place in the church. It will be fun to be all together in one place with the people of the other side.

Individual Cups

The first month passed. At last came the big event, the first awarding of the Individual Cup to the winner from each team. The ceremony was to take place in the church and the Rev-Ref was to award the cups.

On that day, the church was full of hundreds of people. The Balcony Man stood in the middle of the church. He could see the face of his wife. She was smiling. He was this month's winner of the Individual Cup for the Sunnyside. The Referee, in priestly garments, stood at the altar, ready to deliver his Game Sermon and the cups.

The Balcony Man was in a kind of coma. Enid was standing beside him, the cup winner from the Shadowside. He felt asleep and awake at the same time. The people from the Shadowside stood to one side of the church, while the Sunnyside people stood on the other. And Enid stood with him at the center. The Balcony Man knew all those people from the Shadowside. He saw them every evening through his binoculars, and they saw him. Here they looked a little different. Somehow their proportions were all wrong. Binoculars always left some room for the imagination.

The Balcony Man was afraid even to think that Enid was near him. Did people know about them? All eyes were directed toward them. What were they thinking? He looked at each of them. Everybody seemed in a good mood. He did not move. One movement and he would touch Enid, so near was she. He saw the Telephone Gentleman who lived in the flat below Enid's. He saw him every evening, still sitting alone on his balcony. Here, at such a short distance, he looked utterly and wholly unreal.

The Reverend-Referee delivered his Game Sermon, and everyone listened. The Balcony Man could feel Enid listening, motionless as he, as the Rev-Ref spoke.

"We are all human, and all human beings are bound together. The game divides us only for a few hours a day." That was what he said. "The ceremony today will be a symbol of the unity of all men. Will the winners join hands? Will you?"

Would they? For the first time the Balcony Man looked at Enid. Their eyes met for a fleeting moment. And he could not move. Faintly he heard the Rev-Ref say that symbolically the unity of all men all over the world had been expressed before the eyes of everyone. Enid! Enid! In her eyes the Balcony Man could see not only the dream and the fulfillment of all men but also the life-spring of everything which was true and beautiful.

The cups! The cups! He heard applause. He took Enid's hand, and she held his. In the middle of the church. At a sign from the Rev-Ref they started walking slowly up the aisle toward the altar. He saw that the Rev-Ref was holding the cups. Hand in hand they moved forward.

Yes, Enid. I do. I do, Enid. For richer for poorer. I do.

To love, comfort, honor, and serve. I will.

I will serve.

I will, Enid.

From this day forward, to love, to cherish, and to obey.

I do in the presence of God. Yes. I do. To be loving, faithful, and dutiful. Till death us do part. Enid, I love you. In the name of the Father and of the Son and of the Holy Spirit. In the name of the Sunnyside. I will. For better, for worse, in sickness and in health. I do. I do, Enid.

They came before the Rev-Ref, and stopped. The Rev-Ref handed to each of them an individual cup.

Yes. Wilt thou have Enid whose right hand you hold to thy . . . I will. I will. Without hesitation I will. Without looking back. I will. I promise. Till the Game us do part. To take each other, to have and to hold, from this day forward. To be loving, faithful, and beautiful. Oh, Enid. Of course I will. By this accepted symbol of love. Apartment number sixty-six, building six, the Sunnyside! Yes, it is here. It is me. The cup. The cup. Yes. I take. I love. I promise. I declare I will. I do, Enid.

The Rev-Ref had finished counting the points and was giving his reasons for pronouncing apartment number twenty-seven, building nineteen, on the Shadowside and apartment number sixty-six, building six, on the Sunnyside the individual cupwinners for the month. Applause. The world was spinning. The Balcony Man held the silver cup with one hand, his other hand still held Enid's. To have and to hold. To have is to have, said somebody. He looked around. The congregation dispersed, and the sides mingled. It was a very friendly gathering. The ceremony was over. Nobody paid any attention to them. They still stood there holding hands. Someone whispered to him, "Didn't you hear, the Rev-Ref wants to end the ceremony?" Yes? What? Of course. What do I do? "The winners should give each other a friendly kiss to symbolize the love and the sporting spirit which unites both sides." A sporting kiss? Me? Who says so? I didn't hear it . . . Yes. Of course. If the Rev-Ref says so. He knows. In front of all these people? Kiss Enid? Do you promise in the presence of God and before these witnesses to be to her a loving, faithful, dutiful, and beautiful winner? A sporting kiss. No, I can't. I won't. He could hear laughter. Somebody was pushing him gently toward her. He was falling from somewhere flying nowhere. Sport was sport after all. The touch of Enid. Shouts and applause. People were singing. He could not make the song out. People were lifting them. The winners! The winners! Yes. They were the winners, Enid and he. They were separated by the crowd. People from her team were bearing Enid away from him. Her own side was taking her back. Everything was over. Tomorrow would be the balcony. She would be there. She would wait. Friends were surrounding him. Congratulations. Thank you. Thank you. The cup was his. His and yours, Enid. Ours. By this ancient and accepted symbol of love triumphant we take each other to have and to hold from this day forward, for better, for worse . . .

He was carried shoulder high. So was his wife. She was laughing. She was lovely that way, very happy. Everybody was.

That was all for the night. So be it. The end? Enid. I love you, Enid. I know you will be on your balcony and I on mine united by the game. Tomorrow, and after that tomorrow again, and then again tomorrow. Where are they taking me? I love you, Enid. Truly and wholly. Don't run away. Stay a while. Life is not too long. Life is very short. Someone was singing. Till death us do part.

The noise. The people. They chanted and carried him home. With the cup and his wife.

They went to bed. They slept.

Status

For a few days now the Gentleman Who First Discovered the Watching Couple was having trouble with his wife.

In the first few weeks, she and others who played the game derived enormous pleasure in watching others, in discussing their apartments and their habits, in analyzing the relations between the members of each family in question, in guessing their social status, and even in falling in love with the girls on the opposite side.

The trouble started the moment the GD's wife realized that not only did she watch others but, alas, others had been watching her.

When the Gentleman Who First Discovered the Watching Couple entered the bar to have his daily meeting with his two friends, the Gentlemen from the Bar and from the Post, he looked quite disturbed.

"What the hell is the matter?" asked the GB the moment the GD entered the bar. "Are you in love?"

"Don't be ridiculous," said the GD.

"Well, what's the trouble?" said the GP.

"My wife is worried because of our standard of living."

"What?"

"All of a sudden she realized that everybody sees our apartment, our furniture, our TV set, our kitchen facilities, and so on."

"So?"

"She sees other apartments. Obviously she starts comparing."

"So?"

"So, she wants a grand piano, a visible bird's cage with a parrot and a nightingale, and an aquarium with golden fishes."

"You don't say!"

"Why especially a parrot?"

"That's the only bird she couldn't see in any of the apartments on the opposite side. Actually it's the only bird she thoroughly detests."

"Christ!"

"That can't be the case with the grand piano?"

"No. She wants the grand piano because she can see one in the apartment just opposite ours."

"I see. She wants a grand piano because she sees it and she wants a parrot because she doesn't see it. Is that it?" reasoned the GP.

"Precisely."

"And that's the trouble."

"Where am I going to raise the money for all these accessories?" sadly said the GD.

"You'll need quite a lot of funds for all that she sees and for all that she doesn't see," said the GB.

"Besides, imagine how many points you'd give to the other side. A grand piano nineteen points, a parrot ten points, etc. We're always going to lose!" said the GP.

"Unless the women on the other side want to acquire similar things," said the GB.

"The game is going to ruin me," said the GD.

"This is the first time I've felt happy being a bachelor," said the GP.

"To tell the truth," said the GB, "a few days ago my wife also said something, but somehow I didn't pay attention to it . . ."

"What was it?"

"Oh," exclaimed the GB. "Only now I start to see both ends . . . Oh, Jesus Christ Almighty," shouted the GB, "I should have known better!"

"Stop exciting yourself. What did she say?"

"Imagine," said the GB, "she told me she was longing for nature and that she wanted us to move to a place where one sees only green fields, goats, and sheep . . ."

"Nothing wrong with that except that you'd never leave the game."

"That's it. Neither would she. She adores the game," said the GB.

"I don't get it."

"I told her it was nonsense, but she started talking about mountains and springs, the fresh smell of the fields, and the lot. I thought it was just a small nostalgic trip. But, oh, now I understand it all."

"I still don't get it," said the GP.

"At the end she said 'wouldn't it be nice if we built on one of the walls a waterfall, and bought a goat and a sheep to drink from it?'"

"What?!"

"She said it would give her the countryside bit."

"A waterfall? What do you mean by a waterfall?"

"What she meant was a waterfall. A waterfall on the wall!"

"How did you react?"

"I laughed. I thought it was a joke. But she said seriously that I should think it over."

"Did you see any waterfalls in other apartments?"
"Never!"
"Then your wife wants things nobody has," said the GP.
"Did you notice sheep or goats on the opposite side?"
"No. Absolutely not!"
"That's it. It's clear."

The GD felt happier than before. After all, trouble shared is trouble halved. Now that the GB was also confronted with the same problem, he was more confident that a solution would soon be found. The only one who did not share the problem was the unmarried GP.

"I wonder how many families share the same problem," said the GP.

"I bet most of them," said the GD.

"A waterfall in my house!" cried the GB. "On the wall! A water-wall! That's the end of the world! And I didn't even understand the purpose of it!"

"My condolence," said the GP. "What are you going to do?"

"Get the damn status symbols or a divorce," said the GB.

"You don't mean to say that everybody should start acquiring all the damn things or else divorce?" asked the GD.

"That's exactly what I'm saying," said the GB sipping his beer.

"Wouldn't monthly alimony amount to much more than building that water-wall?" asked the GP.

"I don't want a divorce," said the GD. "At my age it would be a disaster. Besides we can always acquire those things in monthly payments."

"Maybe we can rent them or lease them," said the GB.

"We can even make them ourselves," said the GD.

"You can't make a grand piano or a parrot, unless it is a dummy," said the GB.

"I was thinking of your waterfall," said the GD.

"I have it! I have it!" cried the GP. "I have it! I have the answer!"

The GP was dancing holding his glass of beer high above his head.

"What is it, for God's sake."

"Can you play the piano?" the GP asked the GD.

"No."

"Your wife?"

"Even less."

"In that case why should the grand piano be a real one?" asked the GP.

"What do you mean?"

"It can be a dummy grand piano!"

"And a dummy parrot!" exclaimed the GD.

"A dummy everything," enthusiastically cried the GP, "like decor for the theater. No one would ever distinguish between what's real and what's not. It's very cheap too."

"How do you make a dummy of a waterfall on the wall?" asked the GB.

"Like in the opera; a painting of a waterfall with side lights. You see it as if it was real. Through the best of binoculars."

"I never thought you knew so much about the theater or the opera," said the GD with admiration.

"When I was young I wanted to be a set designer but never made it."

"Let's concentrate on our problem," said the GB. "What's next?"

"I think you should speak to your wives and get them to agree on having dummies of status at home," said the GP.

"Don't we have to consult the Rev-Ref?" asked the GD.

"I should think so," said the GP. "I have an acquaintance in the city who is a builder of sorts. I think he also made something for the theater. We could talk to him and see what his suggestions are," said the GP.

"Isn't it terrific," said the GD.

"Isn't that something," said the GB.

It was half an hour before the start of the game. The GB closed the bar and invited the GP to join him on his balcony. The GD happily went home to offer his wife the dummies-status-plan.

It took a week to start the placing of the dummies in the apartments of the two gentlemen. Another week to get the information that people on the other side were greatly impressed by the swift financial success of the two gentlemen, another week for a great number of people to hear about the builder "who was making fake status symbols," and another week for the enormous influx of dummies to sweep the apartments of the housing development.

Arriving home from the city the Balcony Man found a note asking him to get in touch with the Rev-Ref as soon as he could.

After dinner he went to the church where he found the Rev-Ref kneeling before the image of Christ. One could hardly expect anything else. Seeing the Balcony Man the Rev-Ref energetically got to his feet and murmured something about his knees being not as good as they used to be.

"I asked you to come," he said, "in order to discuss certain aspects of the game with you, and to get your advice on some difficulties. Lately a certain trend has emerged," he continued with new spirit, "players, women and men alike, from both the Sunnyside and the Shadowside, have started to be aware of their status, their way of living, and their image as projected to the other side. Some time ago a person from our housing development came to see me. The man in his despair was trying to find a solution for his family that was not divorce. The idea was to build all of the status symbols out of light balsa wood or of cheap plastic and put them in appropriate places round the flat. Here I made my blunder. Here as a man of intelligence I failed. I thought to help the man's marriage and I said it was a good idea as long as it saved their marriage and made them happy. Here I have failed. I gave my consent to the building of a ghost town, where everything can be fake, where nothing has to be what it appears to be. I want to correct the error if possible. Therefore I have called you here to ask for your advice."

For a long time they were silent.

"The rules," said the Balcony Man at last, "the solution must lie there. The rules of the game. Rare wins. Usual loses."

"What do you exactly mean?" asked the Rev-Ref.

"Imagine the following situation," the Balcony Man said. "A certain number of grand pianos, for example, are brought here. Fake or not. Consequently grand pianos become usual. As a result, a grand piano moves from winning points to losing points. The same would apply to any of the status symbols. Now, the moment an unusual thing becomes usual it not only loses points but it also loses status. Status symbols are valuable only when they are the property of the few, or of nobody."

"But how can we determine that an item has become usual?" asked the Rev-Ref.

"The players of each side can count the items in question in the apartments on the other side. You can decide, for instance, that a thousand is the border line between usual and unusual. Every item of the status symbol nature exceeding a thousand would become usual."

"Wonderful solution, wonderful!" exclaimed the Rev-Ref.

"It can work too."

"We can give it a try," said the Rev-Ref.

The Gentleman from the Bar was angry. That night he saw some other waterfalls in various apartments on the opposite side.

Since the dummy waterfall was put onto his wall, he and his wife were stopped many times in the street by players from the opposite side who told them how nice their waterfall was. No one ever doubted it was real. Besides the courtesy of these remarks, there was another meaning. The players on the other side would win lots of points from his waterfall.

And now, seeing these water-walls fast mushrooming on the other side and not being able to tell the fake from the real annoyed him.

The Gentleman Who First Discovered the Watching Couple felt much the same. The many grand pianos, parrots, and aquariums with golden fish, in the apartments on the opposite side depressed him.

Practically in no time every item which had been acquired by the GB and the GD had become usual and, following the Rev-Refs decision, now meant losing points. The two gentlemen, together with the GP, met at once to discuss the new realities.

"My wife is so upset," said the GB. "She can't believe that a waterfall on the wall has no status any longer. Do you really believe there are a thousand waterfalls?"

"You know, I kind of liked the grand piano," said the GD dreamingly. "My wife would sit by it and sort of pretend she was playing it. She always wanted to play the piano, but her parents could never afford one."

"She could go on playing the piano that way, couldn't she?" asked the GP.

"She could do it as long as people believed she was really playing the piano," said the GD. "She cried when one of the women from the opposite side told her in the supermarket that she adored her playing."

"But this woman couldn't have heard any music. How could she say such a thing?" asked the GP.

"Seeing my wife's gestures by the piano, the woman, I suppose, imagined she was hearing music. She also told my wife she had never heard Debussy played with such understanding."

"I see."

"Now that the possibility exists that the piano is fake, it is enough for my wife to give up playing it," said the GD.

"What do you mean playing it? She was only pretending to be playing it," said the GP.

"She *was* playing it. You or some others might have not heard it, but she heard it, I heard it, the woman from the other side heard it."

"You are crazy," said the GP.

"Well," said the GB as if suddenly awake, "I understand what he says. And it's true, believe me. We didn't have a piano but we had a waterfall on the wall. You know, it was made of light nylon strings hung from the ceiling and some side lights. It looked gorgeous. Almost every night when the game was over, we'd draw the curtains and sit in front of it. Then the waterfall was to us as real as any. Sometimes we'd let the water run in the bathtub, for the sound of the water. We felt a young couple again."

"Isn't that funny," sadly said the GP.

"I could put it in a suitcase and keep it there for some other time," said the GB, "but it isn't so nice to put a waterfall in a suitcase. My wife would be broken-hearted."

"Isn't that funny," sadly said the GP.

"What the hell is so funny about it?" said the GD.

"I don't know how to put it," said the GP, "but it's . . . well, isn't it funny to see how a fake becomes real and how a thing made to impress others starts to impress you."

"Yea . . ."

"I still don't understand," continued the GP. "Assume that all these accessories never belonged to the game. Neither points nor status. And you are attached to them as you are now. Who in Christ's sake prevents you from going on having them, liking and enjoying them?"

"A piece of gold," said the GB, "is a piece of gold as long as so many people believe it is a piece of gold. That's a very old truth. I heard it said when I was a child, from a sailor. Do you understand? His wife could play . . . hm . . . what the hell was his name . . . ?"

"Debussy."

"Yes, she could play him so long as others believed they were hearing it."

"I see," said the GP.

"That is what happened with our waterfall. As long as it was real for the others it was real for us too . . ."

"It's damn funny, isn't it? said the Gentleman from the Post.

"It is damn funny," said the Gentleman from the Bar.

"It's not so funny," said the Gentleman Who First Discovered the Watching Couple.

Co-opt The Game!

Little by little the outside world came to hear about the game. And what's more it started to take notice of it.

People from the city began visiting the housing development in the evenings, bringing their own binoculars. They would choose a place on any of the roofs, from where they could see as many windows as possible, and would commence playing the game.

Nobody knew who was the first to offer the visitors chairs, for which they were charged a small amount of money. But as the flow from the city progressed, more and more chairs appeared on the roofs of the buildings. These visitors became known as the Skyside Players. The pleasures of watching others in their apartments and seeing unusual things were for the Skyside Players real thrills. As interest mounted and the numbers of visiting players increased, the Skyside became a factor and a potentiality which could not be ignored.

When the name of the game reached the big cities, as a direct result of the Skyside Players, a network TV news unit was sent to get the story.

Short instructions were given to the crew:

CAMERA I:	CONCENTRATE ON THE BALCONY MAN. BALCONY MAN IS MAN ON BALCONY.
CAMERA II:	INTERVIEW THE GD. GD IS THE MAN WHO DISCOVERS THE BALCONY MAN AND THE WATCHING COUPLE.
CAMERA I:	CUT TO GP. GP IS GENTLEMAN FROM THE PAST. (ASK BLOCK RESIDENTS WHO HE IS.) SHORT INTERVIEW ON FUNCTION IN GAME. ASK: DO YOU REGARD PAST MORE IMPORTANT FACTOR FOR GAME THAN FUTURE?
	NEED TEN-MINUTE FILM. (NET)

Reaching the housing development, the TV unit was thunderstruck. Instead of one Balcony Man, there were hundreds. And the GD who was supposed to discover all these Balcony Men wasn't anywhere to be found.

When they entered one of the apartments, they were thrown out and told to go to the other side. The tenants explained that a TV camera would win seventy-three points for the other side. The other side had the same fears, and so the crew kept moving, from side to side.

Despite their misfortunes, the TV crew brought back an impressive film, accompanied by a brief report in which the TV crew stated: "We could not find one Balcony Man. He does not exist. There are more than five thousand. No one could tell us the whereabouts of the Gentleman from the Past. One man we met claimed to be he. When we checked later, it turned out to be untrue. Nevertheless he said he had long been connected with the game and now was writing a book about it. He started to tell us of a binoculars sale he had managed. He belonged to the past, he said, and therefore was the Gentleman from the Past."

After the ten-minute film was shown on the nightly news, the whole country knew about the game, but hardly anybody knew how to play it. Nevertheless the first seeds of the game were sown and people in many housing developments, projects, and apartment estates throughout the country started to experiment on the basis of what they knew or heard.

In one of the projects, the President of the Chamber of Commerce became the Rev-Ref. In another small housing development the owner of the only supermarket won the election for Rev-Ref, and still in another place, of mostly Jewish residents, the Rabbi was chosen to be the Ref-Ref.

In a newly built project in the south, a couple who first came out onto their balcony to start watching the opposite apartments and by so doing to become the Watching Couple were shot on the spot. The man who shot them became the Gentleman Who First Discovered the Watching Couple.

People in another housing development could not find anybody to fit the description of the Gentleman from the Past, as they had seen him on television. Instead they decided to have a similar, but less romantic title which suited its bearer: The Gentleman from the Post. Knowing they were revolting against tradition in making such changes, they decided to keep the title a secret.

Watching the coverage of the game on TV the Vice President of the OTN (Organized Television Network) realized to his horror that people who played the game did not watch television. It had never occurred to him before. Nor did it to the members of his board of directors. The shocked Vice President called for an urgent meeting.

The members of the board were stupefied. It was true! People who played the game did not watch television. But was it not television which brought the game to the masses? And now playing the game they stopped watching it.

"Co-opt the game!" the Vice President told the board. "If we can't beat them, join them. The game will gain from television and television will gain from the game. Television will offer numerous new possibilities for the game and the game will give television another dimension. I propose to introduce television to the game. I propose to bring television into the game. I propose that we become part of the game. The game as it is played now," continued the Vice President, "is played only with the front windows and the front rooms of the buildings. No one can see the front and the back of the buildings at the same time. But we will show it to them. In one fell swoop they will be able to play not only with the visible front windows but with all windows. Each family will have to have a television set, otherwise it will be quite impossible for them to participate in the game. We are going to co-opt the game!" concluded the Vice President. He rushed out and at once drove to the housing development.

In his church the Rev-Ref was outraged. He had agreed to see the Vice President of the OTN who was coming to discuss the merging of television with the game.

Entering the church, the Vice President was surprised to find there, besides the Rev-Ref, the GD and the GP.

"Everybody's after money and survival," began the Vice President. "Isn't that right?"

"That's all wrong," said the Rev-Ref. "We're not after money. The game has nothing to do with money."

"We want to be left to play the game in peace," said the GP.

"Why does television have to interfere with our game?" asked the GD.

"Let's see," said the Vice President. "You say that money is not involved in the game. First error."

"What do you mean?"

"Because of the game," the Vice President said, "your apartments cost today seven times more than their original price.

To be exact, a rise of 700.30 per cent. The one-family houses in the immediate surroundings went down by almost 30.7 per cent. Some contractors stopped building any other buildings but apartment buildings, in the hope that the game will catch on. In less than two months the turnover of the Fake Status Symbols Enterprise is over one million. The loss of television revenue is due to the game, thus the income of certain people is threatened. How can you say that the game has nothing to do with money?"

"I don't understand. We haven't done a single thing in that direction," said the Rev-Ref.

"I'm sure you didn't, but the discovery of the game did."

"I don't get it," said the GD.

"The game created lots of things which you probably didn't think of."

"So, what now?" said the Rev-Ref. "Frankly, we don't want television in the game."

"I understand," said the Vice President, "but believe me, it's unavoidable."

"But there must be something we could do."

"Accept television. Don't make a war on it," said the Vice President.

"So it's more or less an ultimatum?" said the Rev-Ref.

"It's not I who imposes it," said the Vice President. "It is imposed by circumstances."

"Well, that's that," said the Rev-Ref.

After a number of conferences between the Television People and representatives of both the Sunnyside and the Shadowside, and after a referendum among all the inhabitants of the housing development, it was decided to try the experiment for a period of one year.

The government pronounced the housing development an experimental area and the development received full financial support.

Each family had to have a closed-circuit television monitor on the balcony, which could be switched to twelve channels. Based on careful calculations, twelve cameras (with wide-angle lenses), placed strategically about the housing development, showed everybody the invisible sides of the buildings and their windows.

The game was now played with binoculars on the visible side and with monitors for unseen windows. Players were free to select their own "programs." One could switch to camera seven, for instance, and announce through the loudspeaker system: "Camera seven, two moves, twenty-three points. Binoculars, six moves, fifteen points," and so on.

In this way each of the thousands of players could switch to camera seven and see exactly what the announcer had seen and also the reason for his winning twenty-three points. Anyone who doubted the veracity of the announcer's declaration could ask for a detailed account.

Coin-operated monitors were also placed among the chairs on the roofs of buildings encircling the housing development. The public flocked to take part in the game, and the OTN began considering building high tribunes around the housing development.

Three additional cameras were placed in the housing development to transmit via the national television networks. These programs were called "Highlights of the Game" and became quite popular all over the country.

The Rev-Ref was now delivering his daily sermon to a TV camera. This was transmitted during one of the intervals on all networks.

Almost unnoticed at first, certain companies started capitalizing on the game. The sinking binocular industry was first to make a quick recovery. New models and makes were out in no time. The Glasses with a Soul, the Skyside Binoculars, Binoculars for Men, the Porno Peepers, the Virgin Viewers, and others.

A chain of stores opened calling themselves "Game-It." In Game-It one could get everything for the game. And since everything eventually became connected with the game, Game-It began to sell everything. Game-It clothes, Game-It cars, Game-It foods, and children's Game-It game. The last was a small model of a housing development with two hundred pieces and with everything needed to play the game—flickering lights on the windows, a control system for playing tricks, and lots of miniatures of people and of status symbols. The children's Game-It game became an enormous success. The children who had a Game-It game had class, were hip, and were cool.

New housing developments were springing up. People living in the big cities longed for identical buildings with identical apartments. The price of a single apartment was soon high enough to be worth two country houses on what had been regarded as desirable, tranquil, and solitary parcels of land. Lakes, mountains, and woods were out. Identical buildings of apartments in housing developments were in.

Not only were prices shaken up, people were too. Those who had acquired houses, cottages, and estates in a lifelong attempt to provide security for their families suddenly found all their property losing its value. They were ready to sell at any price. But buyers were not to be found, while flats in the housing developments were virtually unobtainable.

People who yesterday belonged to the upper classes now found themselves speeding headlong toward a different social group. Ideas of prestige were continually being reformulated.

In contrast to the social and financial collapse of the city dwellers, the Game People started to climb the ladder. They began renting out half-rooms, quarter-corridors, thirds of bathrooms, fifths of balconies for the official hours of the game. Bed and Game (BG) notices were springing up everywhere, offering one night's stay with the opportunity to play the game.

It was at that stage that people, at first in small towns and later in big cities, started to revolt against the dissimilarity of their houses.

Because housing and town planning were mostly at the hands of private enterprise, the cities were designed on the principle that one saw as little of one's neighbors as possible. Modern architects worked hard to find new combinations of angle-relations between windows, in order to avoid a direct confrontation between the various apartments. But now, learning that only the dissimilarity of their houses kept them out of the game, people started to search for solutions.

An answer was found in the concept of "reconstruction." This meant enveloping the old houses in wooden frames, all of which were identical to each other. Thus the first condition for playing the game was fulfilled.

These dummy houses had windows which worked on the principle of units. One window in the dummy house could combine a toilet window of one family, half a living-room window of another, and part of a balcony of a third family. These windows, which were cut into the wooden dummies and which joined several families together, served only the players opposite, while the members of the family themselves continued to live and play independently of the exterior imposed on them by the window unit.

Once this answer was found, the reconstruction process got into full swing. The danger that the cities and towns would become grotesque struck some people, who then started campaigning against such a development and urged television to preserve the authenticity of the houses by coming into the game, thus replacing the dummy city and bringing everyone into the game.

This was when the government, together with television,

decided to move into the cities to enable their inhabitants to play the game with the monitor system. Instantly the many wooden dummies were pulled down. Television took over and made it possible for everyone, wherever they lived, to acquire a monitor and play the game.

The game was adapted, shaped, polished, and then exported to the outside world.

The Match

Christmas was approaching. A few days before the Christmas rally, the Rev-Ref received a letter from a boy aged ten. Its contents became known following the Rev-Ref's emotional plea not to play the already planned match during Christmas. The letter read:

> My dear Rev-Ref,
>
> Here is Christmas standing on our thresholds. Today, going down the basement to take my skates from the storeroom I found huge parcels wrapped nicely and carefully. I guessed immediately these were my Christmas presents.
>
> I know I am wrong but I could not stop making a small hole in the paper. Excuse me, but I did it without intending any harm to anybody. After all I am only ten and God will understand. But what I want to tell you is that when I looked into the first parcel I saw that it was a fake present! It was a dummy of a huge tape recorder! I looked at the other parcels and I saw that all my presents for Christmas were fake presents! There

was a dummy telescope, a dummy of the twenty-four books of the Encyclopaedia Britannica and even a huge dummy of a turkey! Specially I cried a lot when I found out that the stereo earphones I wanted so much were not really earphones.

I don't know why the presents are like that, but maybe they are always like that and only one day before Christmas God changes them to real presents. I also thought that maybe they were real and only because I opened them without permission they turned into dummies. I only think this, but I know that it is something to do with the game. My daddy brought home lots of things which are dummies and said they were for the game. I like these dummies a lot. They are fun. But when I saw my presents for Christmas I cried so much and I don't like dummies now.

Because you are the boss of the game maybe you can do something. If you say not to play the game on Christmas day maybe I can get some real presents which I like so much.

Please, don't tell my parents about this letter. I write it privately and I think they can be angry with me.

Don't tell my parents I cried.

The planned Christmas match could not be stopped but the Rev-Ref was organizing a fund for "Christmas Real Presents" (CRP). The response was quite encouraging and he hoped to bring a renewed joy to the hearts of many children in the housing development, by enabling the needy parents to plant among the dummy presents a few real ones.

The start of the Christmas match between the Sunnyside team and the Shadowside team was an hour away. It was to determine the winning of the yearly Challenge Cup. The match was to be the first one to be transmitted by radio and TV.

Ladies and gentlemen, we are just about ready for the start of the great day. Standing with us on the top of the church is the Rev-Ref, who's checking microphones, loudspeakers, and diagrams, minutes before announcing the start of the most important match ever to take place between the so-called Sunnyside and the Shadowside. Tonight the much-talked-of Challenge Cup which is won each year, and this is its first year, will be won by the lucky team. The game will start already with a certain disadvantage to the Shadowside. Because of the semifinal games the Shadowside team comes to this game with fourteen points less than the Sunnyside.

At this moment we are joined by the Captains of both teams.

"How do you feel starting the match, fourteen points behind?"

"As the Captain of the Shadowside team I feel confident and proud of my side."

"What's your forecast for the match?"

"We'll win. We don't have so many Dops and on the other hand we have lots of Wips and Hobbits."

"Can you tell us in a few words what Dops, Wips, and Hobbits mean?"

"Dops stands for Don't Play. People who still refuse to play the game. Wips are Window Pushers, players with excellent sight, who can spot the tiniest details in the apartment on the opposite side, and Hobbits are players trained to adjust the lights or anything else at dicing time to our advantage. Dicing is the time between the throwing of the dice and the counting of the points."

"Do you have any secret plans?"

"No comment."

"Are you allowed to play tricks on the rival team?"

"Sure. It's called Babunka. It can be anything as long as it is within the rules of the game."

"What do you think of the Sunnyside team?"

"They're too busy with facts to deal with fantasy."

"Thank you and the best of luck. Now. Here comes the

Captain of the Sunnyside team. What do you think of the Shadowside team?"

"They're a bunch of Imagists!"

"Imagists?"

"Players who make up things pretending they've seen them on the opposite side."

"What are you going to do about it?"

"We'll ask frequently for VD."

"VD? I beg your pardon?"

"Oh, I see. I didn't mean that! Oh God, that's right. We'll have to change it. In the game VD simply means Via Dolorosa."

"What?"

"Via Dolorosa is the description of the route through the apartments of the rival team. It's an account of what one sees and what makes him win the points he claims to win."

"Thank you and good luck."

Tension is building from minute to minute. Almost all the balconies on both sides are crowded with players armed with binoculars. The balconies are centrally heated and each balcony has its own monitor and loudspeaker. The tribunes and the roofs of the buildings are full of the Skyside team which will have its match tomorrow.

In a matter of minutes the Rev-Ref will announce the start of the game. The players from both sides are observing the apartments on their opposite sides, in order to memorize as many objects as possible and as many details as possible.

Yes! The start has been announced! This is the match between the . . . Oh! Here, we've the first VD, sorry, demanded. Through the loudspeaker you can hear the VD, sorry, of the Shadowside player: "Lands eleventh block, one. Lit, people five. Water-wall, losing nine. Postman enters, one. Thrown out, three. Returns, two. Telegram, seven. Man reads telegram, two. Man gives blow to wife, lose nineteen. Wife returns blow to man, wins twenty-one. Boy enters, one. Reads telegram, two. Man gives blow to boy, lose eleven."

Again VD, sorry, demanded. The Sunnyside is really tough.

"Lands seventh, three. Lit, people five. Postman enters, one. Man reads . . ."

Oh, God! Ladies and gentlemen, we clearly see the trick! The Babunka! The Babunka, which can decide the results of the game. The Shadowside has sent telegrams to all the apartments on the Sunnyside! The Sunnyside is panicking. Later we might hear what was written in the telegrams. Oh! There. Building twelve trying to kidnap the Postman. Is that within the rules of the game? The Rev-Ref announces a penalty of five points for the attempt. The Postman goes on delivering the telegrams.

Now we witness the Sunnyside land on an apartment. We can see that a man approaches the apartment. Well! At last! The Sunnyside have their own Babunka! He brings in a cage with at least ten cats and is freeing them. The Sunnyside is going to win this one! Oh! No! Sorry. What am I saying! Cats is a loser! What? Another trick of the Shadowside! Sending cats to themselves! Oh! Isn't it terrific? Cats! And more cats! The opposite side is losing so many points because of all these cats! Here! The Hobbit is transferring the cats from one apartment to the other. It depends where the landing is. He does it real fast! Is it allowed? The Rev-Ref says—yes! One can deliberately make changes in his own field during game time in order to cause losses to the other side. What a game!

I predict that a game like this will be around for quite a long time. The Sunnyside can't get rid of the Postman who goes on delivering telegrams. Not only that but wherever a Sunnyside player lands, there enters the Shadowside Hobbit with the cats! What a cunning interpretation of the rules!

At the end of the game, after hours of excitement and tension, the Rev-Ref announced the results: The Shadowside was the winner of the yearly Challenge Cup, with seventy-three points ahead of the Sunnyside.

A whole night's celebration followed. Both sides, winner and loser, were united again.

Enid

The Balcony Man walked slowly among the buildings of the housing development. It was late evening but everybody seemed to be still on their balconies playing the game. The only balcony which was deserted was his own. His wife had gone early to bed, and he had decided to stroll for a while. The first stroll in a long time.

What was all this about?

For the first time, the housing development with its astonishing match-box similarity of the buildings looked frightening to the Balcony Man.

Was it the work of a bored architect who could not see anything but straight lines, or of a humorist who had managed to make the only town on earth with all its buildings out of town?

Weren't the virtually identical apartment buildings a reflection of the essence of mankind? Wasn't it only logical that such an environment produced by mankind was apt to go on reproducing mankind in its own image?

Was it the voyeuristic element of the game which hit somewhere at the core of human existence after years of suppressing the human curiosity to watch their own species?

Hadn't the game been always there and one had only to come along and discover it? Was the game a beginning or an end? Or was the game a beginning and end and everything which was in between?

As he walked, the Balcony Man tried to avoid being visible to Enid's balcony. He caught a glimpse of her when passing between two buildings but hoped she had not noticed him.

He thought of the strange development of the game in the last few months. The appearance of television with its monitors, loudspeaker system, and microphones, the ever-changing status symbols which resulted in buy-and-sell confusion, the newly acquired computer placed at the Rev-Ref's church, to determine which of the status symbols had become usual and which had again become rare, the people's addiction to the game and their new life style, and finally the boy's letter to the Rev-Ref.

The Balcony Man thought he was witnessing the creation of a new world the end of which was unpredictable. A child born into it today, he thought, would not even know how simply, how beautifully, and harmlessly it all had begun. Deep inside he believed that the game was heading toward catastrophe. He had started the game but he had not meant it to be that way. It saved his marriage but at the same time it had shown him that love was not at home but across the street. The game showed him love but at the same time thousands of watching binoculars had prevented him from even walking into Enid's apartment. The game pushed television out but then smuggled it in through the back window.

He felt that he was no longer playing the game. He sensed that, contrary to what had been before, the game was playing him and now he did not understand the rules.

Many Skyside Players were still to be seen sitting on the roofs or walking around. The loudspeakers were still in full use. Suddenly the Balcony Man heard someone call after him, "Excuse me, excuse me!" Turning he saw a man with a pair of binoculars around his neck, a normal sight among the Skyside Players.

"Yes?"

"Aren't you the one of the Watching Couple?"

"Yes. Who are you?"

"I don't suppose you know me personally but I was quite well known here at one time."

"I can't recall seeing you."

"They called me here the Lonely Gentleman."

"Oh, sure. The binoculars!"

"That's me. It's great luck for me to meet you. I need you badly. I was commissioned to write a book on the game by one of the best publishers in the country. Can I ask you a few questions?"

"I've nothing to say."

"You invented the game!"

"So what?"

"Aren't you proud seeing all that has happened to your game? All the progress. The modernity of the game. The feel of the new era!"

"I don't know. Really. You better ask someone else."

"The unity of our nation and the gathering around the game!"

"I imagine . . ."

"The enormous progress. At last man has conquered his environment and compelled it to serve him. Don't you see?"

Walking silently beside the Lonely Gentleman the Balcony Man thought that the game had ceased to be a respite from life, a holiday to enjoy. Wasn't it becoming instead a heavy burden resembling what for most people would otherwise be life? Wasn't he himself at the end of his voyage along the twisting turning paths of the game?

"Yes," said the Balcony Man offhandedly.

"There hardly exists any example of such a phenomenon in the evolution of man," continued the Lonely Gentleman. "This is an immense opening into the future . . ."

"Yes."

"Imagine! With television in the game New York could play against Peking, and Moscow against Cairo. People from a small village in Azerbaydzhan could play against people from the island of Zanzibar. People everywhere could play with themselves and with their own apartments. Do you know how many windows there are only in Manhattan for example?"

"No."

"According to my rough account I have come to believe that it's an astronomical number."

"I see."

"Isn't it fantastic?"

The Balcony Man was amused. Was the game finally becoming the main player?

"Do you know," continued the Lonely Gentleman, "what challenges the game poses to man? I mean real challenges. Political, social, economical."

"Yes."

"I propose to carry on international matches and engage the whole world in uniting around the game! Sorry to bother you. You must be aware of all that. After all, you invented the game."

"That's O.K."

"The new system which was created with the discovery of the game is iron strong. One can hardly ever break it!"

"Good night. See you around."

"Please, don't go . . ."

"I have to."

"Please!" pleaded the Lonely Gentleman. "Please tell me if you believed in what I said?"

"It's your opinion, that's all."

"It's not my opinion."

"What do you mean it's not your opinion?"

"It's my act. I wrote it myself and then learned it by heart. I lied to you about the publisher asking me to write a book on the game. As a matter of fact the last time I saw an editor there he almost threw me out, telling me I should come again only if I had something new to tell him. What do you think? Is what you heard O.K.?"

"I don't know. Don't you have an opinion of your own on the game?"

"Of course I have an opinion of my own, but I don't believe in it."

The Lonely Gentleman was crazy. In the mind of the Balcony Man there was no doubt about it. Was it the game-psychosis? Sitting on the pavement the Lonely Gentleman said, "I am sorry. You're so lucky. You have the game. I've nothing."

What a beginning, thought the Balcony Man, and what an end.

Suddenly he felt an unbearable urge to face Enid. Was not she, Enid, of the game?

Minutes after he left the Lonely Gentleman the Balcony Man walked into Enid's apartment.

Seeing him at the door she smiled as if she had been expecting him. She was calm, reassuring and young. Without a word she took his hand and led him inside. Overwhelmed with emotions he could not say a word. Hand in hand they walked through Enid's apartment—the dark corridor, the kitchen, past the balcony and the living room.

Silently the Balcony Man was making his way through Enid's remote little oasis, where she existed, seen by thousands but known by no one. He belonged with her as he had during their walk up the aisle to receive the cup from the Rev-Ref.

To have and to hold . . .

To be to her loving, faithful, dutiful, beautiful . . .

Still without a word, they reached the bedroom. How known and yet how new. Still without a word she took off her clothes and drew him down to her.

Where was the reality of it? He was with Enid . . . in her arms . . . with love.

From this day forward . . .

For better and for . . . better more . . .

They lay together silently. Not a word. Had they not said everything worth saying to each other over so many nights of watching? Didn't they know now that nothing that had been said had been lost on its way between the balconies?

As he looked at her, Enid's eyes were closed in timeless peacefulness. For her the outside world was dead. The thousand nine hundred watching binoculars did not exist. The Balcony Man knew that everybody had seen him enter Enid's apartment. He knew that they had imagined his and Enid's feelings, the pounding of their hearts and the steerings of their bodies as they had walked to the bedroom. There was one window to the bedroom, facing the backside of the building. He did not know if there was a TV camera taking the scene. How many points could he have won for his own side! His wife, he knew, was not on their balcony. She was absent when he, for the first time in his life, had a dream come true. Shouldn't a faithful wife be near her husband at such a moment? Yet she would know of it the next day anyhow, he thought. "We couldn't help noticing your husband's visit to the Shadowside! Do you know her? . . . Oh. Well, they weren't exactly playing the game. But it was good for us that your husband was at the bedroom. We won ninety-one points from it."

"Enid," he whispered.

"Yes?" she whispered back.

"Enid?"

"How do you know my name?"
"I don't."
"But you just said it."
"I said a name."
"It's my name."
"Enid?"
"Enid."
"Impossible!"
"It's true. You knew it, didn't you?"
"No, I swear. I guessed it."
"You're beautiful."
"Is Enid really your name?"
"Didn't you see it on my mailbox?"
"I'll look when I go down."
"You are going?"
"I have to."
"Sure."
"I am leaving the housing development."
"And the game?"
"That too."
"I see."
"I'm sorry."
"Your wife is pregnant, isn't she?"
"Yes . . ."
"Where will you go?"
"Somewhere in the woods near a river or a lake."
"I'll come sometimes to watch."
"I love you, Enid."
"Are you sorry you discovered the game?"
"I don't know. Sometimes I think I am."
"But we had a marvelous time, didn't we?"
"Yes . . . Marvelous."
"You shouldn't be sorry. There are lots of nice things hidden

in the game."

"That's true."

"When your child is born maybe you'd bring him around sometime."

"If it's a girl I'll call her Enid."

"I feel as if it's also my child. We've been together for so long."

"I love you."

"I am happy you discovered the game."

"Shall we go to the balcony?"

"Let's make love once more first."

"Enid."

From mouth to mouth, from binocular to binocular, the word went around. Something unusual was happening. The Balcony Man was at Enid's apartment. It was past midnight and the official match between the sides had ended but quite a few players went on playing individually.

When Enid and the Balcony Man appeared on the balcony, all binoculars were directed at them. For the first time the Balcony Man saw the housing development from a different angle. He could see his own balcony and his own apartment. It felt strange to watch the opposite side and not see an Enid there. He felt that he no more belonged to the game. A game with no Enid on the opposite side was futile. An Enid who would be there whatever happened to the game, whatever happened to one's married life, whatever disasters one met on his way, as the only stronghold, the only element by which one could measure one's own sanity. She had given him strength and had taken nothing in return. For him she was the only sane person left. This balcony had been the only place where he had been able to take refuge from the painful facts in his life. The only place where he had ceased to be a fugitive. A place of rest, a haven of tranquility, amid a chaos of human madness.

He looked at Enid. Standing there looking at the Balcony

Man's empty balcony, she was probably thinking that a game was not a game if there was not a Balcony Man on the opposite balcony.

"Don't be sorry you've invented the game," she whispered.

"I'm sorry it ends this way."

"Why do you go?" asked Enid after a long pause.

"I have to."

"Are you running away?"

"Maybe."

"What from?"

"Everything."

"We might cross each other's track again one day."

"Once I read a book called something like *A Fugitive Always Crosses His Tracks*."

They stood silently for some time.

"Good night."

"Good night."

The night was fresh and windy. Walking, the Balcony Man saw many people following him with their binoculars. Some of the Skyside Players were still around. That's it. Was it the end? It could not be. He looked at Enid's balcony. Seeing her, he waved. She waved back. Suddenly he heard steps behind him. Turning, he saw the Lonely Gentleman trotting heavily toward him. He was drunk.

"I thought you'd never come down."

"What do you want?"

"I must speak to you."

"What's the matter?"

"I wrote some other things for the meeting with my editor . . ."

"I don't give a damn."

"Please, please!"

"Go away."

Walking behind the Balcony Man the Lonely Gentleman was reciting: "The game in its quest for progress would attract the best technical minds of the world. The game is the message. It's going to become a world symbol for a free society and for a new life style."

The Balcony Man began running frantically. He could still hear the Lonely Gentleman shouting, "Enormous resources . . . Money . . . Work . . . The Game . . . The new order . . ."

Entering his apartment the Balcony Man went at once onto his balcony. Enid was already in bed. The Lonely Gentleman went on with his act, still running in the streets.

"Damn it," said the Balcony Man, "damn it all!"

He heard the barefoot steps of his wife but did not turn. She came onto the balcony and put her hands into his.

"I could not sleep much. I'm so excited about the baby."

"Yes."

"What a night."

"Yes."

"Anything the matter?"

"Let's get the hell out of here!"

"I knew that one day we'd have to move out of here."

The Balcony Man looked deep into her eyes. After a long pause he said: "You knew about Enid."

"All along."

"You never said a word."

"Never."

"Why?"

"It was part of the game, wasn't it?"

The next day everybody spoke of the Watching Couple's leaving the housing development. Some said it was because of the Balcony Man's nervous breakdown, others said that his wife needed a rest because of her pregnancy, others said he had an offer to write a book on the game and that he wanted to be some distance from it.

One thing was unexplained. Though the night before hundreds of binoculars had been eyeing him at Enid's apartment, no one even whispered a word. As if in a flash he knew that every single person in that conglomeration of terraced buildings, apartments, and blocks knew all along the one thing he thought was the only hidden corner in his life not exposed to the thousands of binoculars, cameras, microphones, and monitors.

Everybody had long known about Enid.

Suddenly he understood that this mass of people had individually taken upon themselves in silent agreement to unanimously treasure that tiny corner, claiming no part in it. From the beginning they knew he loved Enid, but no one said he knew.

Were they hurt now? The only cause for awakening in them a drop of real generosity was going to leave.

Three days later the Watching Couple left the housing development. They traded the apartment for the isolated villa of the Lonely Gentleman, who gladly moved back to the housing development.

The house was situated in the midst of a small valley surrounded by hilly woods and a river.

The Trump for the Day Was Red

Winter was gone.

Single words, uttered in various places, whispered in corners, hushed in bedrooms, assembled and joined, started to create small trails of rumor: The Balcony Man had invented a new game.

"You are crazy! How on earth can he invent a new game when his house is miles away from any other house?"

"His game is a new game. With different rules. The rules of our game have nothing to do with the rules of his game."

"What are his new rules, then?"

"I have no idea."

"So, how can you say that his rules are not the same as ours?"

"Because if they were the same as ours he wouldn't have left our game to create a new game with just the same rules."

"How do you know he has created a new game?"

"Because his rules are not the same as ours."

"That's true."

"I've discovered something which is unbelievable!"

"What's that?"

"Do you know why the Balcony Man left the housing development?"

"Holy Maria! God Almighty! Don't say it! Say it's not true!"

"It's true. He has a new game!"

"Water!"

"It's my duty to confidentially inform you, gentlemen. He has invented a new game."

"No!"

"There is a new game, you know? Much better than ours."

"It must have many pleasures we don't even know of, this game."

"I'd give anything to know his new game."

"It must be terrific."

"Oh, it is."

"Let me warn you. This meeting is the most secret meeting I've ever called. Good news. Our policy is on its way to being proved right. All the single houses we have bought for peanuts with the bloom of the game might in a matter of months turn into a gold mine. There is a new game played only with single houses. The new game—if promoted right—might cause an enormous influx of people to single houses."

"Oh, baby, don't you think we should get to know the new game?"

"Sh . . . sh . . . Mummy's in the other room. She can hear us."

"Every day he throws a stone into the river."
"Oh, God!"
"And counts the circles it creates in the water."
"What a rule!"

"Did you hear of his main rule? Win the game when a dog barks the exact number of barks as the number of circles in the water."

"Isn't that exciting?"

"Did you hear of the new rule of his game?"

"What is it?"

"You lie on the ground and detect the tallest flower. You pick it up. The color of the flower is the day's trump."

"That's beautiful. A flower game."

"I can tell you most confidentially that in his new game the rules of nature are the rules of the game."

"Do you think he already has all the rules?"

"I don't think so. He is discovering them."

"I wish I knew even some of them."

"Someone told me that yesterday's trump was white."

"Isn't that something. I had my white blouse on yesterday."

"That's right. And I loved you for it."

"White flowers are beautiful."

Without a verbal agreement and without the slightest knowledge of the Balcony Man, people seemed to be weaving, knitting, and constructing the new game.

He did not and could not know that while he had tried to escape the game the game was trying to catch up with him.

One day happily walking along in the valley enjoying the

sun, the spotless blue sky, the clear water of the river, the freshness of the air, and simply being alone, he saw on one of the hills surrounding his house a few people. Somewhat later he noticed a few more on another hill. On the seventh day there were already seven people. During the day he could see them. At night he saw their cigarettes' lights flicker. He started playing.

If after a count of ten there would be an even number of cigarettes' lights he would have a daughter. Uneven, a boy.

Two. Even. A girl.

When there were ten people on the hills the Balcony Man started to detect certain patterns which he thought might be of a new game they played among themselves. They were waving at each other, walking, running, shouting, and lying on the grass.

Each day the number of people grew. One day he could notice a few television cameras and other devices among the people. The once green hills swarmed with people.

Was he becoming the game?

Walking in the valley the Balcony Man remembered that somewhere in the Proverbs was written: "He who troubles his own house shall inherit the wind."

But was it the invention or the rejection of the game that troubled one's own house?

That evening his wife gave birth to a daughter. The girl was born at one o'clock on the tenth day of May.

The next day he thought he saw Enid on one of the hills. He ran into the house and came back with his pair of binoculars.

It was Enid.

Standing in the middle of the valley enclosed by masses of watching people, he whispered: "Oh, God, not again! Damn it! Not again!"

Picking a stone he flung it into the river.

Seven circles appeared on the water.

He took a few steps and picked up a red flower. Everybody knew. The game trump for the day was red.

About the Author

Izzy (Isidore) Abrahami, (1930–2013) was born in Sofia, Bulgaria, and grew up in Haifa, Israel, where he studied agriculture. After the 1948 Arab-Israeli War, he went on to study theater, first in Israel and then in the UK at the renowned Bristol Old Vic Theatre School.

What followed was a mega-tour of capitals and countries—London, Ireland, Norway, New York, Belgium, Israel, and the Netherlands—where Izzy worked as an actor, director, journalist, film and TV director, and artist.

His novel *The Game* was first published in 1973 by Charles Scribner's Sons, and was translated and published in Germany, South America, France, Israel, and the Netherlands. It was also made into a radio play in Switzerland.

His second novel, *Euni, The Book of Enemies*, was published posthumously in 2014, and is based on the author's personal experiences as a teenager during the Arab-Israeli War.

Acknowledgments

Profound thanks are extended to the following for their generous financial support which helped to defray some of this book's production costs:

Ted Adams, Jawad Alhady, Adrian Astur Álvarez,
Matthew Armsworth, Sarah Orr Aten,
Thomas Young Barmore Jr, Nick Barry, Kian S. Bergstrom,
Kurt Beyerl, Matthew Boe, Timothy Bohman,
Brian R. Boisvert, David Brownless, Chris Call, Jeffrey Canino,
Elaine M. Cassell, Scott Chiddister, Chelsea Clifton,
Josh Considine, Seth Corwin, Sheri Costa,
Michael Thomas Costello, Nancy Vieira Couto,
Randy and Haley Cox, Jason Crane, Tyler Crumrine,
Malcolm & Parker Curtis, Robert Dallas, dcmalone,
Frank Derfield Jr, Yenni Desroches, Brian Dice,
Sam & Dylan Doomwarre, Boaz Dror, Johnalbert D. Duverge,
Curtis B. Edmundson, Isaac Ehrlich, Pops Feibel,
Frederick Filios, Robert Patrick Frerich, Stephen Fuller,
Justin Gallant, John M. Gamble, Dan Giancola,
Stephan Glander, GMarkC, Damian Gordon,
David Greenberg, Gavin Greene, Steven Hall, Heather Haskins,
Aric Herzog, Neil Jacobson, Fred W Johnson,
Alex Juarez, Paul Kuliev, Mark Lamb, Samuel Laplante,
Cari Liebenberg, Brian de León Macchiarelli, Jim McElroy,
Donald McGowan, Sean McGrath, Jack Mearns,
Dr. Melvin "Steve" Mesophagus, William Messing, Jason Miller,
Mark Molnar, Spencer F Montgomery, Burke Morton,
Gregory Moses, Irwing Nieto, Rick Ohnemus,
Michael O'Shaughnessy, Tim Owczarzak,

Zach Pattison-Gordon, Andrew Pearson, Lorenzo Sierra Perez, Phlogistina, Ry Pickard, Andrew Pizzey, Waylon M. Prince, Jennifer Pritchett, Judith Redding, Patrick M Regner, Mike Richards, Daniel Roman, Doug Ross, George Salis (www.TheCollidescope.com), Steve Seward, Jake Smith, Jason Smith, Kelly Snyder, Yvonne Solomon, Sid Sondergard, SpongeBama, Jared Stearns, Joel Stimpson, K. L. Stokes, William Edward Stokes, alex tang_96, James D. Teller, Elisa Townshend, Sydney Umaña, Dee W., Zachary Ward, Christopher Wheeling, Isaiah Whisner, Karl Wieser, Charles Wilkins, Brad Wojak, Chris Wolf, T.R. Wolfe, Parker Wright, The Zemenides Family, and Anonymous